CURSING

RIVER WOODS

I0544051

Renaissance
Valley Publishing

Published by Renaissance Valley Publishing

Florence, Alabama
Visit our website at www.renaissancevalleypublishing.com

ISBN: 978-1-7367947-6-0

Woods, River

Contents

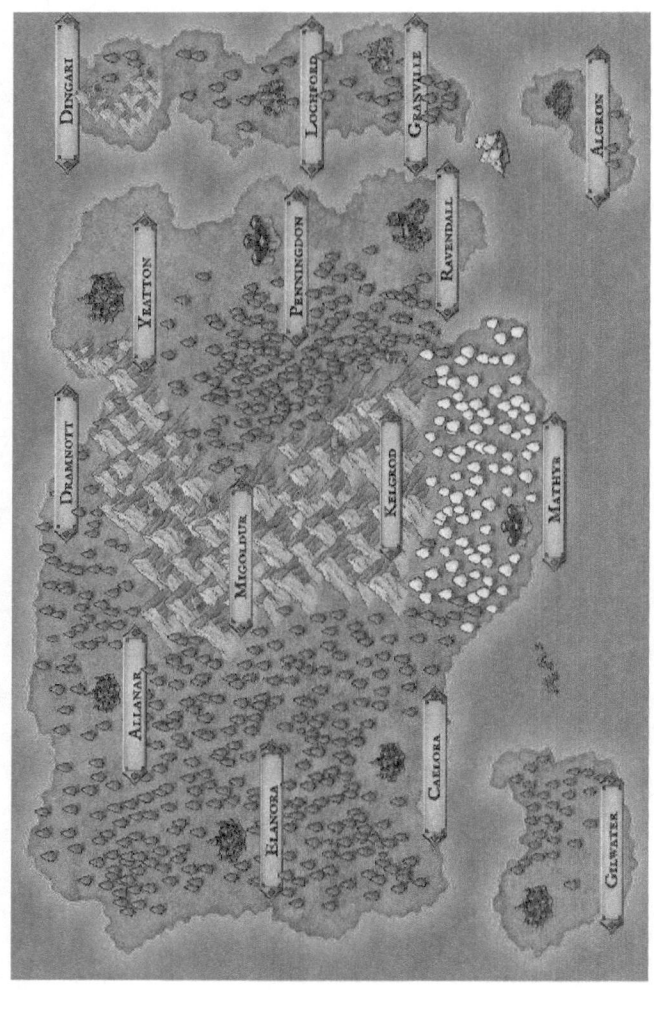

CURSING

Beauty

Chapter 1

Girls glow green when you cursed them. At least, that's what he'd been told. He was about to discover for himself whether that was true or not.

The young elf mage stepped forward from amidst the crowd, his rage burning like an inferno. He had just buried his brother, and the people responsible for his death were celebrating the new life entering their family.

That wasn't fair.

But he could fix it.

He would make it fair. He would make them suffer the same pain he felt. They would soon know the anguish of losing a loved one.

Still, even through the red haze of his fury, he couldn't see the justice of murdering a newborn baby. He would curse her instead. Yes, that would be better, he thought. That way, the king would have years to agonize over the horror that was to come.

All the lords and ladies in attendance had given the baby princess their gifts; now, it was his turn.

As he approached the bassinet, the space seemed to buzz with anticipation. Here was an elf. They were rarely seen on this side of the mountains. It was remarkable, indeed, that one had made the trip to honor their princess.

1

They didn't understand.

They didn't know.

All eyes were on him, and a hush fell over the crowd.

"My gift to the princess is this," the elf said, looking down at the baby. "On her eighteenth birthday, she will prick her finger on the thorn of a rose and fall into an eternal death-like sleep."

The crowd gasped in horror. The king jumped to his feet, but the elf held up his hand. He wasn't finished.

"Only the kiss of true love can awaken her," he said loudly. The guards that had begun to rush toward him stopped to listen.

"But she will never find it. This curse hereby binds her love within itself. Never will she love another, for to the curse alone is she bound."

The elf muttered some words in elvish as the humans looked on in horror. They couldn't move. It was as if the power of the spell held them frozen. Thorn completed his chant and watched in satisfaction as a green glow surrounded the tiny princess.

He turned to the king. "Your selfish actions caused a war that took my brother's life. Now, in payment for that deed, I have taken your daughter's life. I consider us even." With that, the elf vanished.

The courtyard erupted into chaos. Amidst the commotion, the Queen collapsed to the ground in shock. The king knelt by her side, his attention oscillating between comforting his wife and quelling the turmoil around him.

Guards swarmed the area, searching everywhere for the mage, even though it was clear he had gone. Overwhelming helplessness descended on every heart

2

within their ranks. They felt driven to action. Any action. But there was nothing they could do.

The baby princess seemed to sense the tension and began crying in her bassinet.

The elf mage strode through the forest just outside the elven city of Florinia, his mission accomplished.

Princess Elora twisted her long blonde hair into a knot and pinned it at the base of her neck, her mind swirling with thoughts of her upcoming meeting.

She checked the mirror, looking for any escaping strands. Nothing that might reveal her identity could be visible. Secrecy was paramount in case she was seen by a servant or one of the guards. Word couldn't get back to her parents about what she was doing. They would immediately put a stop to it.

Everything looked good. Elora smudged coal powder on the skin around her eyes so it would better blend in with the black mask she would be wearing. How strange it looked.

She stared at her reflection in the mirror.

It stared back.

Their gazes locked, unblinking.

A dull tingle rose up her face, past her nose, and to her eyes. A knot formed in her throat, and her breath felt heavy in her chest. She watched as a single tear escaped her right eye and slowly made its way down her cheek, leaving a coal trail in its wake.

This was not how a princess should look. And secretly meeting a man in her private garden at night was not how a princess should act.

It wasn't fair. Anger toward the elf that had brought her to this state of affairs mingled with anguish at her situation, and a sob tore out of her.

The sound brought her back to the present, and she took a deep breath.

Nope, she thought. *I don't have time to wallow in despair right now. I have more important things to do.*

She would let herself cry as much as she needed to when she returned. If she still felt like it.

Stuffing her emotions into the back of her mind, Elora pulled the black hood up over her head. She rubbed the wayward coal trail off her face and repaired the smudge around her eye. She made one last check in the mirror to make sure her identity was sufficiently concealed.

The black mask hid her eyes and nose, but the hood's shadow barely concealed her mouth. A mouth wasn't terribly recognizable anyway. Was it? Regardless, someone would have to get quite close to her to identify her.

Elora swung her cloak out of the way and climbed over the windowsill. She'd have to be careful coming in and out of her bedroom. The guards couldn't tell who she was, after all. She didn't want to accidentally get shot or stabbed by the very people paid to protect her.

Years ago, she'd asked the gardener to put a trellis outside her bedroom for this very purpose. Not that she'd told him that. He simply believed that she had an obsessive love for honeysuckles. And while she did enjoy their scent, she had no qualms about squashing them when she needed to sneak out of the castle.

Elora quickly climbed down the vine-covered trellis. She'd had a good deal of practice, after all. She

4

had been doing this for years. Ever since she'd first thought of gathering information about the elf who cursed her, her mother and father had forbidden it. They focused on finding someone to break the curse, whether it was another mage or a dashing man.

They claimed that going after the elf, himself, was too dangerous. And maybe it was. They feared him, even though they would never admit it. But she didn't. There wasn't much more he could do to her. Besides, her spies did most of the dangerous work. What could happen to her here in the castle?

Even if the king and queen could be persuaded to target the elf, they certainly would never condone her doing something so rash on her own. And *they* did have more to lose, so she was reduced to this. Sneaking out in the dead of night.

Elora landed lightly and set off across the castle grounds. She had to be quick. She kept to the shadows as she crossed the courtyard, avoiding the torchlight that lined its edges like sentinels.

Elora slipped between the shadows with ease. She moved quickly but silently. She had to duck behind a bush or tree trunk several times as guards walked by, their torches held aloft in their hands like spears in a battle line.

Each time, she silently prayed that they hadn't seen her skulking in the darkness. Finally, after what felt like hours, Elora reached the edge of the palace garden and let out a relieved sigh.

She stepped lightly through the main garden and to the hidden, vine-covered doorway of her personal oasis. She drew her cloak tightly around herself, steeling her resolve as she slipped inside.

Elora scanned the area. The moonlight glinted off the cobblestone path, and the night air was heavy with the scent of more honeysuckles. She really did like how they smelled. Their aroma danced across her nose, and the garden seemed to whisper all around her.

Her heart thudded a little more loudly in her chest, and she could feel each breath she pulled in and pushed out. No matter how often she did this, it never felt any more comfortable.

Exciting. Yes.

But never comfortable.

Isn't that the thing about excitement, though? It rarely goes hand in hand with comfort.

She needn't be quite as cautious here. The guards didn't patrol this place, but still, she stepped lightly. The night was cruel and refused to keep secrets. It would gleefully trumpet any noises, such as the snap of a twig carelessly crushed underfoot, across great distances. Such a thing would send the guards running.

After a few moments of cautious exploration among the flowers and bushes grayed by the moonlight, she spotted her spy. He stood in the center of the garden, his back to her, but as she drew near, he turned.

"I hope you have news for me, Jarden," she said, her voice barely above a whisper.

"I do," he replied gravely. He seemed to hesitate as if weighing his words carefully. "I have just come from the forests outside Allanar. I have a report from our elven spy."

Elora's heart skipped a beat. A wave of anticipation flooded through her. Finding an informant among the elves had been a blessing indeed. "What does he say?"

Jarden took a deep breath. "He says the mage plans to attend a conference in Caelora in two weeks. He should be vulnerable during the trip out."

"Two weeks? That's not much time. We would be pushed to get men in place by then. Do we know when the conference will end? Could we take him on his return journey?"

"Probably not," replied Jarden reluctantly. "He'll most likely use magic to jump back like he did..."

"Like he did when he cursed me," Elora finished for him.

"Yes, Your Highness."

"Are we sure he won't travel to the conference that way?"

"It's doubtful. According to our sources, such travel requires an intimate knowledge of the destination. Without that familiarity, they risk arriving in the wrong place, like inside a tree or rock."

"Ah, yes," said Elora with a snort, "that could be inconvenient for them."

Jarden smirked.

"Where do you think we should intercept him?" she asked. "And how long will it take our men to travel the distance?"

Jarden pulled out a map and spread it over a nearby shrub. Elora could barely read it in the dim light, but it was clear enough for their purposes.

"The safest route through the mountains is Glarendell Pass, provided we don't encounter any goblins. From there, we can ambush him in Evermore Forest, a few miles from Caelora. We should be able to cover the distance in ten to twelve days, depending on how many men we take. If we don't run into any trouble," he added.

"Well, see if you can get enough men ready to go in time. It would be wonderful if we could capture him then. Since he so rarely leaves Florinia, this might be our only chance before the curse takes hold. We'll stay in touch."

Jarden nodded and turned to go.

Elora waited a few minutes in the garden after the spy had left. She sat back on a bench and breathed in the night air, her earlier trepidation having eased somewhat with her newfound hope.

She would have to make sure everything was set up properly. Now that the basic plan was in place, she could communicate with Jarden via messages. If they were to capture the mage, they would have to do it right, or more of them could end up cursed. Or worse.

Her mind raced with plans, contingencies, and possible outcomes. She couldn't afford to make any mistakes.

As Elora stood to leave, she heard a rustling in the bushes, and her hand went to the dagger she had hidden in her belt. She held her breath, waiting to see if someone would reveal themselves. After a moment of tense silence, a figure stepped out of the foliage.

"Who are you?" she demanded.

The figure moved into the moonlight, revealing himself as a man in his late twenties with dark hair and piercing blue eyes. His tunic and breeches were nondescript, not giving away any information about his societal position. Still, his stance indicated he was a fighter—that and the fact that he comfortably rested his hand on the sword strapped to his waist.

"I am Adrian," he said, bowing his head respectfully. "I heard you talking with your spy. I want to help."

Elora narrowed her eyes suspiciously. "What were you doing in my private garden in the middle of the night?"

"I followed your man here from Allanar."

Elora found that hard to believe. Jarden wouldn't overlook someone on his trail for such a distance. He was too good of a forester for that.

The man seemed to sense her disbelief. He held up his hands placatingly. "Don't misunderstand. Your spy is incredibly good at what he does. I never would have been able to go undetected for any length of time if it weren't for a certain special advantage I have."

"And what advantage would that be?"

"Unh uh," he said, shaking his head. "Some secrets shouldn't be revealed so early in a partnership. It robs a person of potential future excitement."

Elora's eyes narrowed even more, and a crinkle appeared between her brows. "Give me one good reason why I shouldn't call for the guards."

"I'll give you two. First, you're not supposed to be out here either. Are you?" he asked with a sly grin. Her lips pursed in irritation.

"And the second?"

"Like I said. I want to help."

"Why would you want to help? I can tell from your accent that you're not from Yeatton."

Adrian stepped forward, his eyes locked onto hers. "No, I'm from Penningdon. But my sister was also cursed by the elf mage. She's been asleep for years, and

I've spent every moment since trying to find a way to break the curse."

Elora felt a pang of sorrow at Adrian's words, and for a moment, her hopelessness resurfaced. "I'm sorry for your sister. But if you've been searching for years, why do you think you would be able to help me now?"

Adrian's eyes burned with determination. "Because I have important connections. What I don't have is soldiers. You have soldiers but not my connections. If we work together, we might have a chance at taking down the elf mage once and for all."

Elora studied him for a moment, considering his offer. She knew it would be risky trying to capture the mage. Her intel only provided dates and general locations. She needed much more information. How many elves would be traveling with him? What were their abilities? Would they have guards?" She studied the man carefully. The crickets chirped in the bushes nearby, and the moonlight gave the garden an ethereal glow.

"What kind of contacts do you have?"

"Elves," he said.

"From Allanar?"

"No," he admitted reluctantly. "From Elanora. They stayed out of the elven-goblin war, so they're much friendlier toward humans. I've met a few who disapprove of our mage friend and how he throws curses around as if they were rose petals." Adrian stepped closer and put his hands on Elora's shoulders, staring deep into her eyes. "They are elves. They can come and go in Allanar without raising any suspicions. They can find out anything we need to know. They can help us get the curse removed."

Elora felt a tingle run down her arms at his touch. Could she trust this stranger? She stared into his handsome face. Was he telling the truth? Was that a dimple in his cheek? Did she really find him attractive? Could it be...?

Focus, Elora, she thought. If Adrian was also fighting for the same cause, it might give her the edge she needed. Elora gently patted one of his hands and backed away from him. His arms dropped to his sides, and she was surprised that she missed the contact.

"Very well," she said. "But we must be cautious. We can't afford to make any mistakes. The elf mage is powerful, and he has many friends. We'll need to plan this carefully."

"Of course."

Elora gave him a small smile. "Good. Do you know where the barracks are?"

He nodded.

"Meet with Jarden tomorrow morning. I'll send him a message, and he'll be waiting for you at the entrance. He'll give you more information about the plan and our soldiers, and you can tell him what you know."

Adrian nodded and bowed before disappearing back into the bushes. Elora watched him go, feeling a strange mix of excitement and apprehension. She had never personally worked with anyone who wasn't from Yeatton before, let alone a stranger. But if it meant stopping the threat that had plagued her family for so long, it was a risk she was willing to take.

As she climbed back up the trellis and into her bedroom, she couldn't help but wonder if this might be it. Could she be close to breaking her curse?

Elora again sat before her mirror, and once again, her emotions threatened to etch a salty trail down her cheek. Just as they had the night before, but she couldn't allow them to escape now. Her maid, Rolena, stood behind her, fixing her hair for yet another outing with yet another eligible suitor. Roe worried about her princess enough as it was. Elora had to stay strong for her sake.

She had to stay strong for everyone. If she broke down, Roe, Deanna, her mother, her father, they would all break down with her. The weight of it was crushing her.

She tried to focus on the constant chatter Roe kept up as she arranged and pinned her hair. Roe was a good friend but not usually such a chatterbox. Elora wasn't fooled. Her maid had noticed her mood and was attempting to cheer her up. Well, she would let her. She could give way to her despair later when she was alone. If she could hold out that long.

"And they say the waterfall at the meadow is beautiful. With the rain we had the other day, it's going strong. You better not sit too close, or the mist might frizz your hair."

Elora forced out a chuckle, making it as light-hearted as she could.

"Maybe I shouldn't," she said with a grin, getting into the spirit of the conversation. "If the duke can't love me with frizzy hair, can he really love me at all?"

Roe stabbed her a little too hard with a hairpin.

"Ow," she protested, raising her hand to her head.

12

"He can love you with frizzy hair after you get married. For now, you need to show him your best side."

Elora frowned. "How about after one month? If we last that long. Can I show him frizzy hair after a month?"

Roe tapped a hairpin against her lips as she thought. "A month might be long enough."

"Long enough for what?" Elora asked with a laugh.

"For him to be so enamored with your beauty that he doesn't notice the frizzy hair."

"Ah. So, what's he like?" Elora examined her fingernails nonchalantly.

"You know I can't tell you that! Queen Callista has made it very clear that you need to meet these men without any preconceived notions." She wagged her finger at the princess through the mirror. "Gossip only serves to make us think the worst about people. It's rare that gossip relates any positive qualities, and even rarer that it relates any truth."

"Yes, of course. You're quite right." Elora nodded seriously. "So. Now that we've gotten the necessary protests out of the way, what have you heard?"

"Well." Roe bent down a little closer and lowered her voice as if someone were listening. "Becky, who works in the kitchen, ran into Martha at the market yesterday. Martha is Duke Ravendell's undercook. She said that he's very excited about finally meeting you. He thinks it's fate that he's one of the last Yeatton nobles to do so."

"Hasn't he been gone for the last five years on a diplomatic mission?"

Rolena nodded.

Elora snorted. "That's not fate. That's just life. He sounds a little dramatic."

"I agree. But Martha said he seemed convinced that he would be the one to win your love. He's even bringing his mother's ring to the picnic in case the situation seems ripe for a proposal."

Elora gasped and turned to face her friend. "A proposal! This is the first time I'm meeting him."

Roe just shrugged and turned the princess back around so she could finish arranging her hair.

"Maybe Mother was right," Elora said. "It might have been better if I hadn't heard this. I'm afraid that I'm beginning to dislike him already."

"Just give him a chance," Roe said, regretting her words. "Martha spoke of him with more humor than malice. If the servants like him, he can't be all bad."

"Perhaps, just a bit dramatic and immature?"

Roe laughed. "You could live with that, couldn't you?"

Elora groaned. "I don't know if I could."

"Well, whatever happens," Roe said, giving Elora's hair a final pat, "you'll look lovely while it does."

Chapter 2

Princess Elora gazed around at the picturesque glade filled with a colorful tapestry of wildflowers swaying gently in the breeze. Sunlight streamed through the trees, casting dappled shadows on the ground. Nearby, a waterfall cascaded down moss-covered rocks, its melodious symphony blending with the chirping of birds.

Elora reclined on a soft blanket, her azure gown flowing elegantly around her. A lavish spread of fruits, pastries, and delicacies lay before her, arranged with meticulous care. Everything looked perfect.

Then she glanced to her right. Duke Ravendell sat beside her. He was younger than she'd expected, no more than twenty-five or twenty-six, with tousled brown hair and earnest brown eyes. He exuded an air of excitement and confidence.

From the moment they had exchanged pleasantries, the duke had been captivated by the princess's beauty. His eyes lingered on her, drinking in her every movement. It was quite annoying.

As were his dramatic compliments and constant attempts to touch her arm, her hand, her shoulder, her anything he could reach. It all made her feel uneasy, though she maintained her composure with royal grace.

"Princess Elora," he said with an exaggerated flourish, "your presence here turns this glade into a garden of pure enchantment."

Elora offered a polite smile, though a faint blush graced her cheeks. "You are too kind, Your Grace."

He reached for a cluster of grapes, his fingers brushing against hers as he did so. "Truly, Your Highness, your elegance is unmatched. Even the flowers seem to bow in your presence."

Elora shifted slightly, subtly distancing herself from him. She turned her gaze to the waterfall, hoping to divert the conversation to less personal topics.

"Duke Ravendell, tell me about your interests and passions," she inquired, hoping for a more meaningful exchange.

His eyes lit up, and he leaned forward eagerly. "Ah, Princess, I am a man of diverse tastes. From horseback riding to the art of storytelling, I find joy in every adventure life has to offer."

Elora nodded, her smile genuine this time. "Horseback riding is indeed exhilarating. I have always found solace in the rhythm of a galloping horse."

The duke's enthusiasm was palpable as he shared tales of his adventures. He spoke animatedly of distant lands he had visited and daring feats he had accomplished. However, to Elora's discerning ear, his stories sounded like they were tinged with a hint of exaggeration, a need to impress.

As the afternoon sun began its descent, casting a warm glow over the meadow, and the duke rambled on, Elora considered the man. While his compliments were flattering, effusively so, they felt insincere and overblown. She didn't think he would be the type to react positively to frizzy hair.

As Ravendell reached for a piece of cheese, his hand brushed against her arm. "My apologies, Your Highness."

Elora managed a gracious smile, her discomfort hidden beneath her royal training. "No harm done, Your Grace."

The moments stretched on, the conversation meandering through various subjects, and Elora perceived that the duke's interests seemed to be driven more by a desire for attention than genuine passion. With a sigh, she decided she could never love this man. Another opportunity gone. Another failure.

Could it be true? What people said about the wording of the curse. Was it really impossible for her to find love?

As the sun cast a warm and golden glow across the glade, Duke Ravendell's demeanor shifted. Elora noticed the shift and began to pay attention to his words again. What had he been talking about?

He gazed at the princess with an intensity that made her uneasy. She softly cleared her throat and glanced away.

"Princess Elora," the duke began, his voice taking on a more serious tone, "I have a confession to make." He reached out and grabbed her hand. Elora tried to pull away gently, but his grip tightened.

Elora raised an eyebrow, curious but apprehensive. "What is it, Duke Ravendell?"

He reached into his pocket and pulled out a small velvet box. Opening it, he revealed a delicate ring with a shimmering gemstone. "This is my mother's ring. It has been passed down through generations, beginning with my great-great-great grandmother."

Elora groaned inwardly. "Your Grace, it is lovely, but perhaps you can tell me of its history later. It is getting rather late." Again, she tried to pull her hand from his grasp, but again, he held firm.

"This will only take a moment, princess. I realize that I have only known you for a short time."

A few hours, thought Elora uncharitably.

"But in that time, I have come to see a woman of unparalleled beauty and grace. Will you marry me?"

Elora's mind raced. She stared at the ring, then at the duke. How could she get out of this one without hurting the poor thing's feelings?

Her eyes met his earnest gaze, and she mustered a faint smile. "Your Grace, I am overwhelmed." She dramatically placed her hand over her heart. If he was going to be overly theatrical, she could be too. "But we have only just met today. Such an important decision requires time and consideration."

Ravendells's hopeful expression wavered, but he quickly masked his disappointment with a smile. "Of course, Your Highness. I understand. I just couldn't help myself. Your beauty and presence overwhelmed me."

Elora nodded, her heart heavy with a mix of sympathy and disappointment. Mostly disappointment. Sympathy for him, of course. But also disappointment in him. Disappointment in the wasted day. Even disappointment in herself.

Some women might appreciate such sudden and effusive devotion. Why couldn't she? Despair flooded her again as he put the ring away, and she waved for the servants to begin cleaning up the picnic. As they returned to the castle, she shoved the emotion aside, once again promising herself relief that night. She just had to make it through that evening's ball, and she could let it all out.

Mage Thornindell Erjeon Greenbow gritted his teeth and tried, for the hundredth time, to focus on the potion he was attempting to make. You would think that after years of dealing with the foolish girl's emotions, he would be able to block them out by now. But the more he tried, the stronger they seemed to grow.

He emptied a vial into the pot and grimaced when the liquid turned brown instead of the expected blue. Turning the vial over, he stared at the label. *Valerium* instead of *Bolarian*. What was he thinking? Clearly, he wasn't. That was the problem.

He slammed the empty vial down on the table with too much force, and it shattered, spewing shivers of glass all over the table and into the mix of herbs he had lying nearby, ruining that as well. With a growl, Thorn threw his hands up and turned away, stalking out of the room and slamming the door behind him.

Anger surged through him. Anger at the human king and queen who had caused all of this. Anger at the human princess whose emotions were a constant frustration and distraction. And anger at himself for making such a vital mistake when casting the curse.

A tiny voice of guilt hovered beneath it all, but he refused to hear it. His actions were justified. He only brought rightful, deserved punishment to those who would otherwise have received no recompense for their selfish and destructive actions.

But the princess was innocent. She had played no part in causing the war, the voice of guilt insisted. *So was my brother!* His sorrow screamed in response. *He was innocent, too!* He fed the pain and anger in his heart until they grew large enough to quash the guilt.

Thorn burst into the training room like a flood. Only two others stood in the corners, practicing their magic. Good. He didn't feel like interacting with anyone at the moment. He created energy ball after energy ball, making them more intricate and powerful each time. The blasts of the explosions caused by their encounters with the wall sent satisfying vibrations through his body.

It required incredible concentration, creating such powerful and complex magic. This was how he dealt with his problems. At first, he had tried drowning his sorrows in drink, but that had only made him do other things to regret, none as significant as his mistake with the curse, but they added up. It had also negatively affected his magic. This release, however, improved his magic. He had the princess to thank for that, at least. No, not the princess. His mistake.

He was young when he cast the curse and a new apprentice. In his attempt to prevent the princess from being able to fall in love, he'd ended up connecting her to himself somehow. It hadn't taken him long to discover his error. And the problems associated with it.

Shortly after he'd returned to his kingdom, he began feeling strange emotions. Foreign emotions that couldn't be his. It was then that he had to admit to Elion what he'd done. Elion, a councilman and the elf to whom he was apprenticed, hadn't taken the news well.

For an elf to curse the child of a human king was paramount to a declaration of war. Under normal circumstances, that wouldn't be a problem. No human army could stand against an elven one. But they were currently at war with the goblins, and their forces were spread thin.

The elven king had gotten involved. Spies were sent out. The situation was monitored very closely. And they waited for retaliation. And waited. When none came, things went back to normal. Perhaps the humans were too afraid to attack. Perhaps they didn't know which elven kingdom he was from and feared to attack the wrong one. Whatever the reason, the elves breathed a sigh of relief.

Elion had studied the curse that Thorn created and discovered what had gone wrong. By binding the infant princess to the curse, he had inadvertently bound her to himself. A curse and its caster are inseparable at the time of casting. That was why he felt her every emotion. And he would continue to do so until the curse was fulfilled, and she slept. At least, they hoped it would stop then. No one could say for sure exactly what would happen when it took effect.

Thorn formed another energy ball, his concentration and rage blocking out the foreign emotions as only they could. Using battle magic was the only activity he could completely focus on. He had learned how to adapt to the consequences of his mistake and use it to make himself stronger. *Not much longer*, he told himself. Her eighteenth birthday was approaching rapidly. Then she'd sleep, and he would be free of her.

His seething fury fueled his magic, taking it to a dangerous level. The others glared at him when the explosion from his last energy ball shook the building. He gave them an apologetic shrug. He wasn't finished yet. He still had a great deal of frustration to expel. He should go outside.

"Do not make a fool of yourself, Elora," Queen Callista whispered forcefully. "People are watching,"

Elora glanced around at the faces of the servants and guards rushing through the corridors. She reluctantly stood upright, pushed her shoulders back and down, and angled her head up, but not too high, tucking her chin.

She was a princess, after all. What did it matter that this was the third ball she'd attended that week? Or that her feet still ached from the walking tour she had taken with Count Milfred yesterday, or that she could be as good as dead in two months if they didn't find some way to stop the curse.

None of that mattered. Apparently, the only important thing was that she stood and walked as a proper princess should. At least the queen had slowed down. That helped.

There should really be a limit to the number of balls one can be forced to attend, she thought as they made their way to the ballroom.

"I'm tired, Mother," Elora said as they neared the Great Hall. The chatter of scores of guests spilled into the hallway. Every week since she'd turned sixteen, her parents had hosted at least two balls in her honor, sometimes as many as four a week. The men in attendance always had to be acceptable young suitors. Surely, by now, she had met every eligible bachelor in the six human kingdoms.

Elora was growing quite sick of the entire process. How was she expected to find love when this whole thing felt like a farce? And she was so tired! The thought alone made her stifle a yawn.

"Focus on this moment, my precious," Callista said, her grip still firm on her daughter's arm. "One night at a time." Elora plastered a bright smile on her face as the attendants opened the door to the ballroom, and they walked in. Her alluring green eyes scanned the crowd like a criminal surrounded by guards searching for escape routes.

The queen noticed her fake smile and frantic look. Her grip on the sleeve of Elora's blue gown tightened so much she was sure to have wrinkled it.

Elora glanced up at her mother. A few curls of dark hair had slipped loose from her updo, and a few small lines framed her eyes, but none of that diminished her appearance. She was always beautiful, the queen. Only the king and Elora could tell how forced her smiles and laughter had been recently. This was draining for her, too. "Smile, Elora," Callista said through her teeth. "And look like you mean it."

Elora forced a more genuine and relaxed smile on her face, the dutiful daughter that she was, acknowledging the scores of men she would have to meet, dance with, and interact with that evening.

Three hours later, she was done. At least fifteen couples still graced the dance floor, but not her. She'd had enough for one night.

As graciously as she could manage, she ditched her last dance partner and tried to sneak out of the Hall. Queen Callista wasn't looking, but the king's voice stopped her in her tracks. "Elora, my daughter." Immediately, she plastered the worn-out smile back on her face. King Leopold only ever called her "daughter" in front of others.

The man beside the king was young and had a pleasant face. Nothing striking, though. He did, however, walk with a certain air that implied that he was used to being revered. Elora couldn't care less.

"Your Highness," the man bowed briefly.

"Good evening," she replied. They hadn't been introduced, so she didn't know how to address him.

King Leopold remedied that error. "Lord Caspian, this is Elora, my daughter and crown princess of Yeatton. Elora, this is Lord Caspian, an earl from our sister kingdom, Penningdon."

Elora rolled her eyes inwardly at that. The king had taken to calling every human kingdom sister—even those across the continent.

"How do you do?" she said to the earl.

"Caspian is a world traveler and has been to many kingdoms and far-off places. Perhaps he'll regale you with his thrilling stories while you dance?"

Elora sighed.

"Your Highness," Caspian stretched out his hand and led her back to the dance floor.

She went dutifully, but she screamed inside. She had already cycled through the usual emotions that she experienced at these events countless times: hope, disappointment, despair, hope, disappointment, despair, hope, disappointment, despair. Now, she was at the exhausted acceptance stage where she felt numb to all else and just wanted it all over with, come what may. She didn't have the energy to start the cycle again that night. No hope came with this new encounter.

"It's a pleasure to finally meet you," the earl said. He tugged on the collar of his tunic, drawing her attention to it. His green and yellow patterned attire made him stand out in the crowd, and she wondered how she had not seen him earlier that evening. If only Deanna had been able to make it to the ball, she would have said something snarky about his outfit to cheer Elora up.

Everyone on the dance floor stopped as the earl and the princess approached. They bowed and curtsied, and the band started a new number. This was another thing she had rapidly grown tired of—the attention.

Subconsciously, she ran her free hand over her gown. Surprisingly, the snug waist, full skirt, and flowing train still looked fresh, even after three hours of dancing. Elora envied its longevity. Caspian's hand pressed firmly on her back, drawing her to the present.

"You are beautiful, Elora," he breathed. She noticed he'd dropped her title.

"Thank you," she said. Yes, she'd been wise to withgo feeling any hope with this one. Her tired legs could hardly keep up with his flamboyant moves.

"So, you are a traveler," she started when he said nothing else.

He spun her in a dizzying circle as he replied, "I am not one to talk about my adventures on the dance floor. But anything for you, Elora."

The familiar way he said her name grated on her nerves.

"There are many beautiful places outside Yeatton," he said. "For example, there is Ravendall, just a three-day ride away. It is rumored that there is painite in its soil."

"Interesting," she said, trying to stifle a yawn.

"And they make the finest silk. This cost me an arm and a leg, but it was worth every coin, don't you think?" Pride radiated in his voice.

"Have you encountered any other species?" she asked, changing the topic.

His face turned sour at that. "You mean the elves and goblins and whatnots." Disgust saturated his tone.

"Yes, them." She was genuinely curious. Mainly because one of them was responsible for her predicament, and any information she gleaned could be used in her pursuit of the mage.

The earl sneered. "If I ruled the continent, I would have them all banished along with every book or story mentioning them. A filthy lot, they are."

His aversion to the other species intrigued her. She could understand a disdain for elves, but what did he have against the others? Before she could ask, the dance ended.

Her need for the comfort of her rooms outweighed any intrigue he created.

"Thank you for the dance. Have a lovely evening," she said quickly as she backed away. He stopped her with a tight grip on her arm. The impatient expression on his face morphed into one of exaggerated tenderness.

"Elora," he said, bringing his face close to hers. She could feel his breath on her nose. It was uncomfortable, to say the least. "This has been the best night of my life. It has been a dream come true," he said.

"Er, it was a pleasure," she replied politely, her eyes darting around for an escape route.

"I do not want it to end just yet. I want to spend more time with you."

"Unfortunately, the dance is over," she said.

"We could do something else." He puffed out his chest and licked his lips. "I am sure you are also not ready to part company with me," he said. Irritation broke through her exhaustion. Why couldn't the man take a hint and just let her leave? But he wasn't done.

"You have the most beautiful green eyes, Elora," he said, brushing his hand down her cheek. She flinched at the touch. "They sparkle like emeralds in sunlight. I can't have them, but our children would."

Elora coughed at that. *Our children? Deanna will laugh her insides out when she hears this,* she thought.

"Marry me, Elora." He said seriously. "You and I would rule this great kingdom together."

"I'm sorry, no," she said, stifling the laughter bubbling in her throat. How gullible and desperate did he think she was? "There won't be any marriage between us."

He had not expected that response. He blinked repeatedly, running his fingers through his hair. "Wh-wha-what do you mean?" he stuttered.

She did not give him a response. Instead, she pulled away and joined the guests spilling out of the Great

Hall. The earl was too stunned to stop her. Elora was glad the queen had not been there to witness it. Though she knew she would hear about it before the night ended.

She spotted Deanna talking to a guard by the stairs leading to the private quarters. She would recognize her reddish-brown hair anywhere. She made to go to her, but a voice stopped her.

"Your Highness."

Elora sighed resignedly. Would she ever have her own time this evening?

"Her Majesty, the Queen, requests your presence in the Throne Room," The courtier bowed as she delivered her message.

"Thank you."

It wasn't difficult to guess what she wanted.

The queen stood by the wall behind the thrones, staring at their family portrait. Elora joined her. Her eyes examined the painting. She had been younger then, barely sixteen, just before the frantic search for a husband had escalated. She looked happy. How naïve she had been.

"Ah, Elora," Queen Callista said sweetly. Hope flickered in her eyes. "Is it done?"

"Is what done?" she asked warily.

"The earl," she replied. "Did you fall in love with him? He seemed quite charming,"

"There's nothing with the earl, Mother."

King Leopold chose that moment to join them.

"What do you mean?" The queen's voice sounded broken, and Elora hated being the cause of it. "He seemed so perfect."

"The earl wasn't a match?" King Leopold asked.

"He asked me to marry him, and I refused," she said pointedly.

"Did you even take your time to get to know him?" Callista asked. "It shouldn't be so difficult."

It really shouldn't, even though one dance was hardly sufficient time. Though her parents and the entire kingdom had been trying to find someone for her to fall in love with, it was never right. She couldn't click with anyone. There was never anything there. Except... She thought about her meeting with Adrian in the garden. There had been something. Only the tiniest of sparks, but that was more than she had ever felt with anyone else. Could it be possible?

"We are running out of time, my love," Leopold said quietly. "The curse cannot be broken if you don't fall in love before your eighteenth birthday. That's less than two months away."

A fresh wave of despair flooded her body, warmth and pressure filling her. Tears welled up in her eyes as she beheld the dejected faces of her parents.

"I know," she said hopelessly. "I know how important this is. I wish I could snap my fingers and make it happen, but I can't. Maybe what the elf said is true. Maybe I'm not capable of feeling romantic love."

Her mother sighed heavily as her father enveloped Elora in a hug. Tears coursed down her face as she hugged him back.

"May I go now?" she whispered into his jacket.

"Yes." He held her shoulders briefly, then pulled out a handkerchief and wiped her eyes. "We'll see you tomorrow."

Elora nodded and hurried away. She kept her head slightly bowed and pulled some of her hair loose to partially conceal her red eyes. She was aware of the consequences if she didn't fall in love. Everyone was.

When Elora got to her room, Roe instantly picked up on her mood. She knew her friend and princess well enough to understand she wanted to be alone.

The maid quickly helped her out of her dress and into her nightgown and quietly shut the door behind herself as she slipped into the hall. Elora flung herself across her bed. She hid her face in her pillow and gave in to the pressure of the knot in her chest. She poured out her despair and sorrows in great shaking sobs.

Chapter 3

The sun shone brightly in the sky, and a light breeze wafted through the trees in the nearby orchard. People chatted amicably as they walked to and fro, going about their daily chores.

"You know," Deanna said as she ambled across the castle courtyard with Elora. "If your mother and father really wanted you to fall in love, they should expand their search to men outside the nobility."

Elora raised her brows. "Such ideas, Deanna. I am a princess." She imbued every word with the utmost haughtiness.

Deanna rolled her eyes and laughed. "Perhaps, but you're not blind. Look over there and tell me I'm wrong."

Elora swiveled her eyes to the barracks training ground. Deanna was not wrong. Scores of well-built, muscular men went through their training exercises. Shirtless. She certainly felt something while watching them, but she couldn't honestly say it was love.

"I've often wondered how long it would take Mother to branch out," she said. "She is very strict about the rules she believes royalty should follow, but her desperation could eventually lead her to expand her search."

Deanna snorted. "Well, if she's going to do it, she better do it quickly. You've pretty much exhausted the pool of eligible noblemen under the age of sixty."

"You're forgetting Lord Pendrick. He was sixty-two," Elora reminded her friend as they leaned against the fence that enclosed the training arena.

"Oh, yeah. That's right. I'd forgotten about him. Why had he been included? He was a pompous, boring old thing."

"Deanna!"

"Don't get me wrong. I've met some older men that I think a younger woman could be happy with. It's not his age that I object to, though it did seem a bit inappropriate. It's his personality. He was awful. I can't understand why your mother thought you could love him."

Elora watched the men sparring, their bodies glistening with sweat and their muscles rippling with their efforts. "I think it was because of his stables. He has excellent horses. Maybe she thought we could bond over that shared interest."

"She is getting desperate, isn't she?" Deanna replied. Her words were weighted down with sorrow; in them, Elora felt the worry and fear her friend so often tried to hide. She didn't respond. There was no need.

"Here comes your biggest fan," Deanna said with a smirk.

Elora glanced to the side and saw Jarden approaching. She needed to talk to him alone. She had never told her friend about her plans for the elven mage. She trusted her in all else, but this... Deanna's concern for her well-being would make her feel she had to inform the king and queen. Besides, this could be dangerous, and she didn't want her friend getting hurt.

"You know," Elora said. "Perhaps you're right. Maybe I could find love among these fine soldiers."

"Well, this one appears to like you. He seems to take every opportunity to talk to you."

Elora panicked for a moment. Had they been so obvious? She turned her face toward the approaching man to hide the fear in her eyes. "Well, he would be a good place to start then. Could I have a little privacy?"

She heard Deanna chuckle behind her. "Sure," her friend said as she casually strolled farther down the fence to watch another group of soldiers fighting.

"Adrian and I have coordinated," Jarden said quietly as he approached. "We should have everything ready to go tomorrow at dawn."

"How many can you take?"

"Only thirty."

Elora nodded. She had hoped for more, but it was enough.

"What excuse have you given the guard commander?"

"I may have somewhat embellished the trouble brewing across the mountains when I returned from my last mission. It's possible he thinks the elves could be preparing for an attack on us. He's given me permission to take the men and investigate further."

Elora stifled a laugh. "That's good. Is there anything you need from me? Anything I can do to help?"

Jarden smiled at her and shook his head. "You can't come with us if that's what you're thinking."

That was exactly what she had been thinking, but he was right. There was no way she could get away with it.

"I know that," she said stiffly.

"Just leave it to us, Your Highness. We will do everything in our power to catch this cretin and force him to break the curse."

Elora gave him a weak smile. "I know you will, Jarden. Thank you. Be careful."

He nodded and walked away.

Deanna instantly appeared by her side. "Well, any love sparks?"

Elora laughed. "No, no love sparks for me, but..."

"But what?" Deanna narrowed her eyes suspiciously.

"Well, he is quite handsome and a great warrior. I think the two of you might make a good pair."

Deanna glanced at his retreating back thoughtfully. "Hmm. Doesn't he like you?"

"Not particularly. He just wanted to know if we needed anything. He's very loyal and polite."

Her friend narrowed her eyes suspiciously. "Really?"

"Uhm hum. Look! He's going to fight Urick."

"Oh!" squealed Deanna. "He's taking off his shirt."

Elora laughed at her enthusiasm. If she couldn't find love for herself, maybe she could help her friend find it.

Among the ancient trees of the elven realm, the morning sun cast a golden hue upon the treetops, illuminating the bustling activity within Thorn's grand treehouse. The air was alive with the scents of moss and dew-kissed leaves, a refreshing reminder of the forest's vibrancy.

Inside, Thorn stood next to a sturdy wooden table in the center of a room strewn with trinkets of magic and memories. Before him, lay a map, its corners curling slightly from the touch of time.

Beside him, the vibrant Lyariel hummed a lilting tune as she meticulously folded his mage robes into a well-worn leather satchel. Her auburn hair cascaded down her shoulders in waves, and her eyes sparkled with an unquenchable enthusiasm.

Across the room, Edrym leaned against the wall, muscular arms crossed, a half-smile playing on his lips. His long, silver hair fell like a waterfall, adding an air of elegance to his rugged features.

Thorn examined the map, tracing the path with a practiced eye. "We should reach the convention within three days if all goes smoothly," he remarked.

Lyariel looked up, a mischievous grin playing on her lips. "Smooth journeys rarely make for interesting stories, Thorn."

Edrym chuckled. "True enough. Remember when we got caught in that storm near the Crystal Peaks?"

Thorn snorted, "Ah, yes. You thought you could shield us from the rain with a simple spell. You made it worse instead, and we ended up stuck in a downpour that lasted hours."

"Wait a minute," Edrym protested, moving his hands to his waist. "You're the one that cast that spell."

"Nope. It was you," Thorn insisted.

"Was it?" Edrym glanced at his friend quizzically. "Hmph. Well, we all make mistakes."

Thorn chucked and turned his attention back to the map. As he rolled it up and carefully stowed it in a tube, the door creaked open, and Captain Thalir entered. "The others await near the stables. It is time to gather."

Lyariel tossed her satchel over her shoulder and grinned. "To the Mage Convention!"

Thorn tightened the straps on his own satchel, his thoughts drifting to the challenges ahead. Would he be able to control the pesky princess's emotions while they were out among strangers? They wouldn't understand if he suddenly reacted strangely in a meeting. He would have to, he told himself sternly.

With their belongings secured, the trio ventured outside to the bustling scene near the stables. A couple of guards in elegant armor stood at attention, their expressions stoic and alert. The three other mages attending the conference stood nearby, chatting animatedly, robes billowing in the breeze.

Among the mages, Elowen, a spirited woman with silver hair and a penchant for transformation magic, caught Lyariel's eye and waved her over. "Lyariel! Edrym! Thorn! It's good to see you. I can hardly wait to see what new spells we'll encounter at the convention."

Edrym chuckled, and Lyariel grinned back at Elowen. "You know that with your affinity for shapeshifting, Elowen, you'll be the highlight of the whole conference."

A middle-aged elf mage with a long, silver beard approached them, his staff glowing faintly with arcane energy. "Thornindell, Lyariel, Edrym, I trust your preparations are complete?"

Thorn inclined his head respectfully. "Indeed, Elder Arannis. We are ready to depart."

Elder Arannis smiled warmly. "Safe travels, my friends. May the winds carry you swiftly, and may your wisdom be well-received at the convention."

The group mounted their steeds – sleek elven horses with coats that shimmered like moonlight.

The sun painted the forest in golden hues, and Captain Thalir's voice rang. "Move out."

With a glance exchanged among them, they set off, and the forest enveloped them. The fragrance of pine and earth intermingled, a soothing balm to their senses.

Lyariel turned to Elowen. "Any new spells you hope to learn?"

Elowen's eyes twinkled. "A few offensive ones, perhaps. They might come in handy since I'm not as good with a sword as the three of you are. "

"I'm looking forward to the lectures on advanced elemental magic," Lyariel said, her eyes alight with curiosity. "They say the fire mage from the Eastern Enclave will be speaking."

Thorn nodded in agreement. "And I hear the library at the Caelora is unrivaled."

Lyariel's lips curled into a grin. "Do you think you might be able to find anything that will help with your predicament?"

Thorn grunted. "Not likely, but it wouldn't hurt to try."

"I've heard rumors of an artifact exhibition," Elowen added. "I'm curious to see what's on display."

Thorn's eyes gleamed. "Artifacts from different realms—that should be interesting."

As they neared a meadow, the sounds of a distant waterfall reached their ears, and the birds joined their songs to the deep bass of its far-off roar. Thorn turned to watch the sunlight as it glimmered off the dew-covered flowers.

"While you three indulge in academia, I plan to test my skills in the sparring arena. I heard a renowned blade master is attending," said Edrym, interrupting his musings.

"You know..." said Elowen mysteriously. "Speaking of who's attending. I heard a rumor that the Elanorian group was bringing some human mages."

"What! Can they do that?" asked Edrym.

"They wouldn't dare," added Lyariel.

Elowen raised her brows and tilted her head. "That's what I heard."

"Well, if that's true, at least the conference won't be boring," said Lyariel.

"You can say that again," added Edrym.

Thorn scowled. This was not good. He had a difficult enough time controlling the princess's emotions. If he added his own anger to the mix, there was no telling what might happen. This was a bad idea.

That night, Thorn and his companions made camp in a small clearing. The scent of pine and earth enveloped their weary bodies, and the crackling campfire glowed with warm hues and sent sparks dancing into the night sky. Thorn sat, watching the flames frolic, his lavender eyes reflecting both the fire's glow and the depths of his thoughts.

As usual, the princess's emotions were strong that night. They were often the most potent after darkness fell. Based on the nature of the feelings, he could only surmise that she was at a social gathering and being subjected to a barrage of suitors.

Thorn smirked. He had heard rumors of the king's search for someone she could love. It was futile. He had made sure of that. But that didn't stop them from trying.

If only they knew what torture he endured at these attempts, they would probably think their efforts were at least somewhat successful. He buried the emotions as deeply in the back of his mind as he could. They never went away completely, but at least he had become adept at subduing the mild ones. It was the extreme emotions that still overwhelmed him.

The first day of their journey had been both exhilarating and exhausting yet, thankfully, uneventful. The sun had long since dipped below the horizon, casting shadows through the ancient trees of the forest. Their elven eyes enabled them to travel through the dark with little trouble. Their horses, on the other hand, could see in the dim light better than most breeds but still couldn't travel through such thick darkness that this night in the forest held.

Beside Thorn, some of his mage companions gathered in a circle around the campfire while their two guards, Valen and Selene, stood watch on the perimeter, their vigilant gazes scanning the darkness beyond.

Lyariel, her auburn hair now slightly tousled from the journey, grinned as she passed around a pot of hearty vegetable stew. "Ah, the first campfire feast of our journey. There's nothing quite like it."

Edrym, who had a knack for finding comfort even in the wild, leaned back against a fallen log as he accepted a wooden bowl. "Indeed, Lyariel. This forest seems to welcome us."

Thorn agreed. "It's a good omen. Perhaps we'll have a safe journey."

A comfortable silence settled over the campsite as they ate, the forest around them alive with the gentle rustle of leaves and the occasional hoot of an owl.

Lyariel leaned back, her bowl now empty. "It's nights like these that make me love traveling. Don't get me wrong. I love our forest city, but there's something about being away from the noise of the crowds."

Edrym laughed. "If you think our cities are loud, don't ever visit a dwarven or human city."

Lyariel wrinkled her nose. "I might not mind visiting a dwarven city, but who would ever want to go to a human city? I've heard they're nasty places full of foul odors, disgusting filth, and, yes, noise."

"And don't forget humans," added Edrym. "They are also full of humans."

"Yes, and humans," Lyariel agreed with a sneer. "I didn't mean to say that Florinia is anything like that. But you must agree that even it is not as silent and peaceful as it is out here." She waved her hands, indicating the surrounding nature.

Edrym's gaze shifted to the stars. "True, true. The stars above us, the trees around us—the Evermore Forest is like a living tapestry woven with magic."

Elion, a hint of wistfulness in his voice, added, "And the stories whispered in its leaves, carried by the wind."

Thorn set his bowl aside. "And what stories would those be, Elion?" he asked with a grin.

With the campfire's warm embrace wrapping around them, Elion leaned forward, his eyes alight with the anticipation of sharing a tale passed down through generations of their elven kin. The crackling firelight cast playful shadows across his features, turning his every expression into a dance of light and shadow.

"Listen closely, for the story I'm about to tell you is one that echoes through the very heart of the Evermore Forest."

The group's gazes never wavered as they watched Elion's eyes, their curiosity as palpable as the night air that rustled the leaves around them.

"Long ago, in the days when our people's connection to the elements was stronger and our bond with the forest unbreakable, there lived a young elven maiden named Lireth. She was known throughout the forest for her radiant spirit and her ability to converse with the creatures of the land. Her laughter sounded like the tinkling of bells, and her every step left a trail of blossoms in her wake."

Elion's voice took on a melodious quality as if the words themselves were enchanted to tell the story.

"One day, as Lireth wandered deeper into the heart of the Evermore Forest, her heart felt unusually heavy. She followed a path of fallen petals until she came upon a clearing bathed in an otherworldly light. In the center of the clearing stood a magnificent tree, its bark as silver as the moon's glow, and its leaves shimmering like stars."

Thorn's brow furrowed slightly, captivated by the image Elion painted. "What kind of tree was it?"

Elion smiled softly. "It was a Tree of Echoing Dreams—a rare and ancient tree said to be a bridge between the realms of the waking world and the realm of dreams. The tree's magic allowed those who listened to its whispers to glimpse the stories of the past, present, and even the future."

Thorn's eyes widened in wonder, his curiosity deepening with every word. *A bridge between the waking world and that of dreams?* He thought. Did such a bridge exist?

A shudder shook him. If such a thing were possible, could it further complicate the error he made with his curse? If it truly offered glimpses into the future, maybe he could use it to find answers.

Elion continued, and Thorn listened intently. "Lireth approached the tree with reverence, her heart pounding with excitement and trepidation. Visions flooded her mind as she laid her hand upon the tree's silver bark. She saw the laughter of children, the whispers of lovers, and the battles fought by heroes long forgotten. But among those visions, one stood out—a lone figure standing at the edge of a precipice, gazing into the unknown."

Lyariel leaned in, her voice barely a whisper. "Who was the figure, Elion? What did it mean?"

Elion's gaze held a depth that seemed to transcend the present moment. "The figure was you, Thorn." His eyes locked onto those of the shocked elf. "And the precipice represented a choice, a pivotal moment that would shape the destiny of our people and the entire world."

Everyone stared at Thorn in surprise and wonder. His breath caught, and his eyes searched Elion's face for answers that seemed just beyond reach.

"Lireth, shaken by the intensity of the visions, knew she had been given a profound gift. With the Tree of Echoing Dreams as her guide, she embarked on a journey to uncover the truth behind the visions, to understand the threads that connected them all."

The fire crackled, its flames mirroring the flickering images that danced within Thorn's imagination.

"As she journeyed through the forest, Lireth encountered creatures, both mythical and mundane, each with a piece of the puzzle to share. She learned of ancient treaties, mutual respect, and collaboration and peace between our people and the other species, peace that began to unravel due to growing discord between them all."

Thorn's eyes glistened, a realization dawning upon him. "The choice I had to make in the vision—it was about mending that peace, wasn't it?"

Elion nodded, her gaze unwavering. "Yes, Thorn. The choice before you is to bridge the divisions that threaten our harmony or to allow them to spread. Just as Lireth listened to the whispers of the Tree of Echoing Dreams, you must listen to the stories carried by the wind, the wisdom shared by the stars, and the lessons whispered in the leaves."

Thorn frowned and glanced around the circle. The eyes of his friends had all grown wide and were glued to his face. "So, what does that mean?" he said. "Am I supposed to forgive the human king and try to break the curse I put on his daughter? It wasn't that act that shattered the peace. It was the human king who did that."

Elion held up a placating hand. "No one is blaming you for what happened. You're right. If the human king

43

hadn't claimed the mountains as his domain and began populating it, the goblins would not have been forced out of their homes. And if the goblins hadn't been forced out of their homes, they never would have attempted to take over our forests, and the war would never have started. You played no role in that."

Thorn smiled tightly, feeling somewhat vindicated.

"However," Elion continued. "Your curse did increase tensions." He patted him on the arm. "You cannot deny that."

Thorn frowned but reluctantly nodded. "Regardless, I can do nothing now even if I wanted to. The curse can only be broken by true love's kiss, and I made sure the princess could never love."

"Not exactly," Edrym said.

Thorn glared at his friend. "What do you mean?"

"It's not that she can never love. It's that her love is bound to the curse."

"Isn't that the same thing?" asked Lyariel.

"No," replied Elion hesitantly. "I'm not sure what the difference is, but there would be a difference."

"Ha!" Edrym slapped his knee as he laughed. Everyone stared at him curiously.

"What's got you so tickled?" asked Lyariel.

"I just had a thought." His smile spread as he soaked in the attention.

"Well, will you share it with us?" asked Thorn.

"You know how when you bound her to the curse, it caused you to feel her emotions? Because the curse and caster are one when the curse is being cast." His eyes danced with laughter.

Thorn gasped as he began to understand.

44

"What?" asked Lyariel, glancing back and forth between the two.

"Since he bound her love to the curse, and the curse and caster are one, doesn't that mean that he bound her love to himself?"

"No," said Lyariel breathlessly. She struggled to stop the smile that threatened to overtake her face. It wouldn't be sensitive to find humor in this situation, not when her friend could be so adversely affected by it.

Elion nodded wisely. "That is possible."

Lyariel, with a mischievous glint in her eye, turned to Thorn. "So, would that mean that the only person she could love would be Thorn?"

Thorn sat frozen, staring into the flames. Clearly, he was in shock.

Elion's gaze remained steady. "It would appear so. If our interpretation of the curse's wording is correct."

"Don't worry about it, man." Edrym slapped Thorn on the back, breaking him out of his stupor. "It'll still produce the same result as what you intended. It's not like you'll ever meet this girl, and even if you did, true love has to work both ways. She might be bound to love you, but that doesn't mean you'll ever love her." He wrinkled his nose in distaste at the thought. "She is a human, after all."

The fire crackled, casting sparks skyward like stars caught in a momentary dance.

"That does seem a little unfair," said Lyariel sadly, breaking the silence.

"What do you mean?" asked Edrym.

"I mean, it doesn't seem right that the princess is forced to love someone she's never met. That she doesn't have any choice in the matter. And an elf at

45

that. People who hate her." The men watched her curiously. Was she siding with a human?

"I'm just saying, there's no telling who she might have loved if the curse had never entered her life." She looked around at them. Their faces reflected everything from surprise to disgust to sternness.

"Yes, I know she's a human, but she's also a woman." Lyariel shrugged. "I just feel a little sorry for her, that's all."

Thorn stood without a word and walked away, silently disappearing into the trees.

They all watched him go.

"I understand what you are saying, Lyariel, and if Thorn is honest with himself, he can understand, too," said Elion. "In time. But I think you may be mistaken on one point. I don't believe the wording of the curse would force the girl to love him. I think, instead, that he is the only one she could love. Whether she loved him or not would depend on her alone."

"Not that she'd ever get the chance," pointed out Edrym. "As I said. When will they ever meet? She'll fall under the curse in less than two months, and his worries will all be over."

"Will they?" asked Elion, his brows raised.

"You know," Edrym said, changing the subject, "I've always wondered why the goblins moved into our forests instead of fighting the humans for the mountains. Even with their fewer numbers, their magic would have given them more of an advantage over that inferior species than it does over us. They most likely would have won quite easily."

"They didn't want the mountains," Elion replied. "Millennia ago, they actually lived in the Greendell Forest."

"Really?" Lyariel asked, surprised. "What happened?"

"The elves won it in battle." Elion shrugged. "The goblins have always wanted it back. This was the perfect opportunity for them to take it. The actions of the human king provided them with an excuse and the perfect justification, at least in their eyes."

He rose to his feet and raised his arms over his head, releasing a great yawn. "I am beginning to grow weary. I think I'll turn in. Goodnight, everyone."

Lyariel's eyes scanned the surrounding trees.

"Don't worry," said Edrym. "He'll return when he's ready. I think I'm going to get some rest, too." He glanced back at his friend as he walked away. "Good night."

Lyariel leaned over and stoked the fire, its light casting dancing shadows across her face before she, too, headed to her bedroll.

Chapter 4

Princess Elora sat gracefully on a plush cushioned seat, her fingers delicately tracing the intricate patterns of her teacup. Across from her, Sir Percival droned on about his bug collection, his voice a monotonous hum that barely reached her ears. She kept a serene smile on her lips, her eyes drifting to the vibrant garden beyond the open windows. The sweet scent of blooming flowers teased her senses.

She wondered where Adrian and Jarden were now. They'd left ten days ago. They should be arriving at their destination soon if they weren't already there.

"And you see, Princess, the iridescence of the elytra on these jewel beetles is truly a marvel of nature," Sir Percival intoned, his eyes gleaming with an enthusiasm that failed to ignite any reciprocal interest in Elora. "The manner in which they refract light, displaying a rainbow of colors, is a testament to the intricate beauty woven into the fabric of our world."

"Indeed, Lord Percival, it sounds utterly fascinating," Elora replied politely, her gaze still lingering on the petals that swayed in the gentle breeze. She sipped her tea, the delicate porcelain barely registering in her hand.

Percival's face lit up, encouraged by her response. "Ah, but that's not all, my dear Princess. Allow me to regale you with the tale of the rare Golden Glimmer Beetle. Its habitat, deep within the heart of the Evermore Forest, remains a sanctuary untouched by the passage of time. Legends say its wings hold the secret to eternal illumination, a beacon of hope for all who seek enlightenment."

The mention of Evermore Forest took Elora's thoughts back to the mission. Percival's words became a distant hum. She imagined the forest with its enormous ancient trees and the Golden Glimmer Beetle soaring through the dappled sunlight, casting a golden glow upon all who crossed its path.

Then blood.

Splattering its red hue across the bright flowers. She shuddered. Surely, it wouldn't come to that. Jarden had planned his ambush well. They should be able to take the elf with little effort—and little bloodshed.

Percival leaned forward, his eyes narrowing with intensity. "You know, Princess, the meticulous process of preserving these specimens is an art in and of itself. It requires a delicate touch, a keen eye, and an unwavering commitment to preserving their splendor for future generations."

Elora's attention flickered back to Percival as he lifted a magnifying glass to inspect a mounted specimen on the table. She observed the beetle's intricate details, its tiny legs suspended in a pose of eternal movement. In about a month and a half, that could be her. Frozen for eternity. She controlled the shudder this time, but she felt the familiar tingle make its way from her nose to her eyes.

No! she told herself firmly. She was not about to break down here in front of this man. She forced the tears away and attempted to focus on this oh-so-fascinating suitor.

"Truly, your dedication to this endeavor is admirable, Sir Percival," Elora offered, her voice as warm and appreciative as she could make it.

He beamed at her compliment, encouraged to continue his monologue. "I must admit, there have been nights when I've lain awake, pondering the intricate symbiotic relationships between beetles and the flora they call home. The delicate balance of nature's tapestry, woven with threads of adaptation and survival."

Elora felt a yawn building and tried to swallow it.

"And do you know, Princess, the study of beetles has led me to explore entomology's profound connection to broader scientific inquiries?" Percival's eyes gleamed with fervor as if he were on the precipice of unveiling a world-changing revelation.

Elora's curiosity was piqued slightly. "Pray tell, Sir Percival, what connections have you discovered?"

He leaned in, his voice hushed with a conspiratorial tone. "The adaptations of beetles have influenced engineering feats, inspiring innovations in architecture and design. Their exoskeletons, a marvel of lightweight strength, have inspired the creation of more durable and efficient materials for our own creations."

Elora understood the importance of such connections and realized the intelligence of the man before her. He would be a worthy partner to someone who shared his interest. Unfortunately, that person wasn't her.

"How about this one?" Deanna popped out of Elora's closet, holding a mint green day dress out for inspection.

"Hmm." Elora walked over to it and felt the fabric. She pressed her finger against her lips and examined it critically, twisting and turning it to see every side.

"Oh, good grief," Deanna huffed. "It's perfect. Don't you agree, Roe?"

"I have always liked that one."

Elora laughed. "Of course. You know I trust your judgment. It's beautiful."

"Then, let's get you into it," Roe said as she began undoing the laces of Elora's morning dress.

"So, who's it going to be this afternoon? Any ideas?"

Deanna and Roe looked at each other.

"I actually haven't heard anything," the maid said.

"Me neither. You mean you don't know?"

"No. That's odd." Elora's voice was muffled by the yards of fabric being pulled over her head. "I wonder who it could be. My parents aren't usually so secretive about the identity of my suitors. Their personalities, yes, but not their identities."

"Maybe they've finally branched out to the other species," Deanna suggested.

Elora and Roe froze.

"What do you mean?" asked the princess.

"Do you think so?" asked the maid at the same time.

"It would explain the secrecy."

"Surely not. There's got to be another reason," argued Elora. "It is entirely possible that there is no secret. We might just not have heard."

"I would have heard," said Roe. "Gossip like that is difficult to quell completely. No, whoever you're about to meet with, their identity is definitely being kept a secret intentionally."

"Maybe it's an elf!" Deanna's eyes lit up.

"Why does that thought excite you?" asked Elora defensively. "In case you've forgotten, elves are the bad guys here."

"I know; I know. But you can't deny that they are incredibly attractive."

Elora heaved a great sigh. "They wouldn't dare."

"No, you're probably right. A goblin, then?"

"That's almost as bad," argued Roe as she laced up the new dress. "Have you forgotten we recently drove them out of their homes? I doubt they would treat our princess with much gentleness."

"An ogre?"

Elora hit her friend's arm. "An ogre? Really, Deanna? Those guys are huge. Not to mention frightening. And grumpy. I doubt they would risk it."

"A merman, then."

Elora laughed. "Where would we live?"

"I know," said Roe as she ushered the princess to the dressing table. "A dwarf."

"Hmm," considered Elora. "That could work. I wouldn't mind a dwarf. They seem normal enough, though I'm not crazy about the beards."

"Maybe he would shave for you if you asked nicely," said Roe as she pulled Elora's hair back into a simple braid.

"I don't know," said Deanna, drawing her words out, "dwarves are really fond of their beards." She picked up a pillow and twirled it in her hands. "You might have to ask very nicely." She pressed her lips to the pillow passionately, making exaggerated kissing sounds.

"Oh!" Elora grabbed a perfume bottle and threw it at her friend. Deanna raised the pillow just in time to avoid being struck. It bounced off the soft shield and landed harmlessly on the bed. Deanna laughed.

"Don't you go breaking that perfume bottle," said Roe in a huff as she rushed over to retrieve it. "Do you know how hard it is to find this scent?"

"Sorry, Roe." Elora smiled sheepishly at her friend.

"So, do you think that's who it is?" asked Deanna, plopping down on the bed. "Your new suitor. Do you think he's a dwarf?"

"Who else could it be?"

A knock on the door sounded as Roe finished tying the bow at the bottom of Elora's braid.

"I guess you're about to find out." Deanna jumped off the bed and opened the door.

A footman stood outside.

"The king wishes to see you in his office, Your Highness."

"Thank you, William. I'll be right there." The girls stared at each other in surprise.

"In his office?" Elora slid her feet into her slippers. "That's an unusual place to meet a suitor. What do you think is going on?"

The other two just gazed back at her helplessly. They had no clue.

Elora's heart sped as she approached her father's office. It was rare that the king summoned her here. Except at the beginning when he had every mage in the six human kingdoms examine her. Was that all it was? Had her father found another mage, or maybe one of the original ones had returned with some good news.

That thought sent a surge of endorphins through her that put a bounce in her step. She hurried to the door and waited impatiently as the guard knocked on it and listened for the king's command to enter. The moment the door opened, she rushed inside, her excitement morphing into fear at the sight before her.

Three goblins stood beside her father's desk. She had never seen a goblin before, but there was no mistaking what they were. Their skin, a slightly darker hue than her own, was lightly tinged green, and their ears were pointed only a bit longer than an elf's. Other than that, they appeared surprisingly normal. One of them might even be considered handsome. A chill ran down her spine. Could one of them be a suitor? That would certainly explain the secrecy. The people would not accept this easily. Especially since whoever she married would become the next king.

"Hello, father," she said hesitantly. "Did you want me?"

"Yes, Elora." The king walked over to her, hands outstretched. When he reached her, he pulled her to his side, his arm around her back like a brace holding her together. "Allow me to introduce you to Mage Vrek and his companions, Bral and Briq.

A mage! Elora let out a breath she hadn't realized she held and allowed herself to relax. Not a suitor, then. This she could handle. This was familiar. But goblins?

"Gentlemen, this is my daughter, Princess Elora."

She curtsied politely. When she looked back at them, all three men were staring sharply at her. After a momentary pause, they bowed back.

"She is quite lovely," said Mage Vrek. "I hope I will be able to help her out of this distressing situation that those abominable elves have put her in." His lip raised with a snarl at the word 'elves.' There could be no doubt regarding the animosity between the two species.

Mage Vrek continued, his gaze now fixed on Elora's eyes. "If you allow us, we would like to examine the curse more closely and ask you some questions about the details before trying a few magical remedies to break it."

Elora nodded, grateful for the opportunity. "Of course, I will try anything to escape this curse."

Mage Vrek motioned for Elora to sit at the desk while Bral and Briq stood silently by his side. The room seemed charged with an unusual energy, a mixture of anticipation and apprehension.

The goblin mage began a series of questions, delving deeply into the specifics of the curse's effects, the circumstances of the encounter with the elves, and the nature of the magical bindings.

Elora didn't know the answers to any of the questions. She felt herself sinking into the usual despair that followed every surge of hope. Mage Vrek appeared disappointed but not surprised at her lack of knowledge on the subject. She, however, was a little surprised. She had studied so much about curses and thought she had learned a great deal. It seemed, now, though, that she hadn't learned anything worthwhile at all.

When the questioning was done, Vrek turned to a collection of scrolls he had laid out on the desk, carefully unrolling one that contained intricate symbols and incantations filling the entire surface.

"We shall start with a simple dispelling spell," Mage Vrek announced. He began to chant in a language that resonated with power. A soft, ethereal yellow light enveloped Elora, causing her to hold her breath anxiously. But as the last word of the incantation left Vrek's lips, the light dissipated, and the curse remained unbroken.

She knew.

She could tell.

She had felt the weight of it ever since she could remember. And that weight remained.

Undeterred, the goblin mage moved on to a vial containing a shimmering blue potion. "This potion has been known to counteract certain elven enchantments," he explained. Elora trustingly drank the tincture, but again, the curse's grip remained unyielding.

Two more spells followed, intricate weavings of magic and eldritch words. Elora's heart raced each time with renewed hope, only to sink again as the spells proved ineffective. Frustration was etched on the mage's face, his brows furrowing as he exchanged hurried whispers with Bral and Briq.

After a moment, Vrek straightened, his expression determined. "We have more theories to test, but they require time and controlled environments. Would it be possible for us to stay within the castle for a while, continuing our experiments in seclusion?"

King Leopold hesitated, glancing between his daughter and the goblin mage. "I understand the urgency of the matter," he said, "but the presence of goblins within the castle would be met with resistance from my people."

"We understand," Mage Vrek replied. "We are well-versed in concealment spells. If you can give us an out-of-the-way place to work, we can remain hidden, and only you and your daughter need to know of our presence."

The king sighed, his shoulders slumping as he weighed the options. Finally, he nodded. "Very well, you may stay. But if anyone discovers your presence, it will not only jeopardize your safety but also the safety of my daughter."

Mage Vrek and his companions bowed deeply in gratitude. "Thank you, King Leopold. We shall do our utmost to remain hidden and work diligently to break this curse."

As her father ushered the three men out the hidden passage in his office, Elora couldn't help but wonder what was in it for them. Did they think the king would reward them with her hand in marriage? Did a goblin want to become king of Yeatton? And if so, why?

The moonlight filtered through the dense foliage of the forest, casting an eerie glow on the thirty-two men as they moved silently through the underbrush. They had smudged their faces with dirt and dulled their armor to avoid reflecting any light. Jarden signaled for them to halt, his hand raised in a clenched fist.

"Spread out and take your positions," he ordered in hushed tones. "Remember, the mage from the picture must be taken alive. Do whatever you need to do to the rest of them."

The soldiers nodded grimly and dispersed, each finding a spot behind trees and rocks, their weapons at the ready. They had set a makeshift trap in the center of the ambush—a taut net woven with enchanted rope that would immobilize anyone who stepped into it, even a mage.

Adrian leaned against a tree beside Jarden. "We should have someone hidden farther down the path to tell us when they're coming."

"Matthews is stationed in the tree one hundred yards south." Jarden kept his eyes focused on the said tree.

"Do you think that's far enough?" asked Adrian.

Jarden turned to him. "You do not? It is the standard distance."

"Whatever you think," said Adrian with a slight bow.

Jarden cocked his head to the side. "What is standard practice in Penningdon?"

"We usually station someone at least a mile down the road. If the enemy has gotten wind of anything unusual, they will likely fan out from that distance."

Jarden narrowed his eyes at the man. "There is no reason to believe the elves will have gotten wind of anything. This mission has been conducted in strict secrecy."

"Of course," Adrian agreed. "But then…"

"What?"

"Well, they are elves and mages at that. Who knows what tools they have at their disposal."

Jarden pressed his lips together. "Very well. You'll take that position. Keep an eye out and let me know as soon as you see anything."

Adrian nodded and disappeared into the trees.

In the depths of the forest, Thorn and his companions rode on, chatting pleasantly, unaware of the danger that lurked ahead.

Suddenly, a slight rustling in the distance drew their attention. It was too loud to have come from a small animal that far away and too uneven to have come from a large one. Thalir raised a hand, signaling for everyone to halt. They listened.

"A person," he said. The group slid off their horses and pulled out their weapons. Lyariel and Elowen sat in the middle of the path while the men hid behind the trees. The girls loved playing the role of bait. Most species underestimated them, and it was always fun to teach them a lesson.

A few moments later, a human man emerged from the underbrush. The elves immediately surrounded him, the sharp points of their weapons resting against his chest and back. He raised his hands in a gesture of peace. "Wait! I'm not your enemy. I've come in peace."

"Peace, human?" asked Elion. "You sneak up on our party in the middle of our forest, and you speak of peace? Who are you?"

"My name is Adrian. I'm here with soldiers from Yeatton. They've set up an ambush for you a couple of miles down the road," he panted, clearly out of breath from his hurried journey through the forest. "I came to warn you."

The elf companions exchanged glances, their skepticism evident.

"Why?" asked Edrym. "Why would you betray your own people to warn us?"

Adrian's eyes sought out Thorn. "I know about the curse, and I know what happened to your brother. Now that the princess is so close to her birthday, the king wants revenge for what will happen to her. He sent these men here to kill you all."

Thorn studied him carefully.

"And I couldn't do it. I couldn't be part of that. I'm no fool. I know how this would end. If humans kill you, then your people will retaliate. Then, another war will begin, and thousands will die. Please, you have to believe me. I just want it all to end."

Thorn's grip on his blade loosened slightly, his instincts telling him that Adrian was at least partially speaking the truth. Something about his story felt off, but Thorn believed the ambush, at least, was no lie. "Tell us everything you know."

Adrian quickly recounted the ambush plan—the net trap, the number and positions of the soldiers, and Captain Jarden's orders with a slight adjustment. "They are to kill everyone they have to, but the king wants a few survivors to take back to the castle so he can have them tortured, and he wants one of those to be you," he said to Thorn.

Elowen gasped, and Adrian gave her a sympathetic look.

"I volunteered to watch for your arrival. That's how I got away without them knowing."

"You say you are tired of the bloodshed, but you must know we cannot avoid this battle. We will not. And now that you have warned us, we will have the advantage. Your comrades will die today. Are you at peace with that?"

A frown slowly grew on Adrian's face. "Maybe it is for the best," he said. "If they kill you, a war could start, but if you kill them, after all the preparations they have made, they will have to acknowledge that you are too powerful for them. They wouldn't dare try again."

"You think so?" asked Elion.

"I think so." He didn't sound as sure as he had a moment ago, but it was enough.

"Very well, you have possibly saved our lives. What can we do to repay you?" asked Elion.

"If all goes well for your party, I ask only that you remember me and the favor I have done for you this day."

"Agreed."

With a last glance at the elves, Adrian melted back into the forest and took up his position with no intention of giving any warning to his brothers-in-arms.

Chapter 5

Captain Thalir led his group from the alcove where they had been hiding for the last few hours. As elves, they would have the advantage in a night battle, and darkness had finally fallen.

They made their way through the forest, their senses keen to any hint of danger. When they drew near the first sentry, Thalir raised his hand, commanding the group to halt. His eyes scanned the area, and his ears tuned in to the sounds around them. He could hear the breath of the sentry only a short distance away.

Satisfied that Adrian's information appeared correct, he signaled half of their party to go around the ambush site to the right and the other half to the left.

The elves moved with the stealth of shadows. The forest seemed to embrace them, concealing their motions as they separated into the two groups—one poised to attack from the front and the other slipping silently through the underbrush to approach from behind.

The tension in the air was palpable, the energy of the impending clash sizzling. They reached a point where they could see the hidden soldiers. The men appeared less alert than they should have been—another benefit of waiting until nightfall.

And then, in the span of a heartbeat, chaos erupted. Thorn's group surged forward, their swift movements a shimmering dance of magic and steel. Spells crackled through the air, arcing like stars, and the clash of weapons rang out in a chaotic symphony.

The element of surprise was their greatest weapon. The human soldiers, caught off guard, scrambled to respond. Arrows flew, swords clashed, and the forest echoed with shouts and the eerie hum of magic.

Thorn's sword, an extension of his will, danced with deadly precision. His magical strikes seared through the night, each swing leaving trails of stardust. Lyariel's voice rose in a melody of power, conjuring fiery swords that blazed with an intensity that matched her spirit. Edrym's hands crackled with lightning, causing arcs of electricity to strike the soldiers.

Thalir, his years of training evident, moved seamlessly, his hand flowing smoothly from his quiver to his bowstring and back again, his arrows finding their marks with uncanny accuracy.

The second group emerged like apparitions from the shadows behind the human soldiers. Elion's spells swirled with vibrant hues, searching out and finding the humans hiding in the trees.

Thaldrin's ice crystallized the air, freezing the ground beneath the soldiers' feet and their weapons, slowing their movements. Elown, in a whirlwind of transformation, bewildered the soldiers, causing them to hesitate as wolves, birds, and other creatures moved among them. And Salin's strategic strikes disrupted their ranks, making them lose cohesion.

The battleground became a vortex of magic and steel, illuminated by the moonlight and the flames of the skirmish. The elves moved with an otherworldly grace, their unity and power overwhelming the human soldiers.

Captain Jarden spun just in time to see the elf they had been hunting, the very elf who had cursed his princess, charging towards him with a raised sword. Thorn's lavender eyes blazed with determination and hate, his long brown hair streaming behind him like a forest banner. Jarden's fingers tightened around the hilt of his sword, his stance poised and ready.

Thorn's steps were swift, his movements fluid as he closed the gap between them. An ethereal haze formed around him as if he were one with the wind that rustled through the trees. Jarden braced himself, his sword steady as it met Thorn's in a clash of steel against steel. Jarden's skills were honed, each strike executed with precision, yet Thorn wielded something more—the raw power of the elements.

Thorn summoned fire to his aid with a flick of his wrist, the flames leaping from his fingertips to dance along his blade. Jarden's eyes widened in surprise, but he didn't falter. He parried the fiery strike with a well-timed block, his sword sparking as it met the enchanted weapon.

Jarden moved with a fluid grace that spoke of years of training. His strikes were a dance of exactitude, each movement calculated to disarm and disable. On the other hand, Thorn fought with a raw, primal energy that drew from the elements around him.

Thorn's eyes narrowed as he channeled his magic, shifting the air to his advantage. A gust of wind erupted around them, carrying swirling leaves and debris that obscured Jarden's vision.

Thorn seized the opportunity, his fire-imbued blade cutting through the space in a deadly arc. Jarden barely managed to dodge in time, the flames licking at the edges of his cloak.

Jarden's heart pounded in his chest, adrenaline coursing through his veins. He swung his sword, aiming for Thorn's exposed flank. But the elf mage anticipated the move, summoning a wall of earth from the ground beneath his feet. The wall rose like a natural shield, intercepting Jarden's strike. Undeterred, Jarden advanced again, determined to test Thorn's prowess. He lunged, swift strikes aimed at exploiting any opening.

Thorn's breath quickened as he faced the renewed assault. The sound of clashing swords echoed in the air. The fire-imbued blade met Jarden's steel in a dazzling display of combat.

With a growl of frustration, Jarden swiftly switched tactics. He dropped low, sweeping his leg out in a low arc, aiming to knock Thorn off balance. The elf mage leaped into the air, his body moving with an uncanny grace.

Water formed from the mist in the air at his command, transforming into a torrential wave that surged towards Jarden. The captain's eyes widened in surprise as the wave crashed over him, drenching his clothes and soaking his boots.

He stumbled backward, his footing compromised by the sudden onslaught of water. But he didn't relent. He pushed through the wave, his determination unwavering as he closed the distance once more.

Thorn again summoned the earth beneath him, this time causing the ground to tremble. Jarden's balance wavered, and in that instant, Thorn released a torrent of flames from his hands. The inferno engulfed Jarden, his armor absorbing the brunt of the attack, but the heat of it forced him to his knees.

Jarden quickly caught his breath. With a fierce cry, he lunged forward, his sword finding its mark as it sliced across Thorn's arm. The elf mage gritted his teeth, his blade faltering momentarily as pain coursed through him.

As Jarden moved to attack again, Thorn's fire blade radiated with intensity, flames blazing as they met Jarden's unyielding defense. The fire blade cut through the air, slicing across Jarden's chest with a searing burst of fire. He staggered back, his vision swimming as the flames licked at his armor. The armor held though the heat made it searingly painful, even with the layers of his shirts separating it from his skin.

Then, with a final clash, Thorn's fire blade met Jarden's sword one last time, shattering the steel as if it were glass. The force sent tremors through Jarden's arms, causing his grip to falter. Jarden stumbled back, his strength waning, his armor scorched. Thorn's fierceness shone in his eyes, flames reflecting their intensity.

Jarden's broken weapon fell to the ground, his hand releasing its grip. His chest heaved with ragged breaths, pain radiating through his body. Thorn stood before him, fire blade still ablaze, fatigue mingling with triumph in his gaze. Jarden slid to the forest floor, his body weakened and battered. As darkness began to overtake him, he saw the elf mage turn away to face another foe. And in that moment, as his consciousness faded, he thought only of his princess.

As the fight raged on, Thorn's group pushed forward, their attacks unrelenting. The human soldiers, outmatched and outmaneuvered, began to falter. Their formations began to crumble; their attacks grew less coordinated. The magic of the elves wielded a dominance that could not be denied. Realizing the futility of their situation, the surviving human soldiers retreated, dragging their wounded captain with them into the depths of the forest. The elves let them go.

Thorn and the others stood amidst the aftermath, their breathing heavy, their faces illuminated by the glow of their magic. Thorn's gaze swept the clearing, taking in the fallen soldiers and the fading traces of their spells.

His companions gathered around him, their faces a mixture of exhaustion and triumph. Thorn met their eyes. "We stand as one! Against any odds!" he said, raising his sword high, his voice carrying the weight of their shared victory.

Princess Elora took a deep breath and savored the various aromas of the market. It was so rare that she could be out and about alone. Well, sort of alone. With the guards trailing behind her, she was never truly alone. But this was as close as she had come in a long time.

The bustling city was alive with activity, merchants hawking their wares and villagers going about their daily business. Elora scanned the colorful stalls, and her fingers brushed over the exquisite fabrics and beautiful jewelry on display.

It was a nice temporary escape from the constant social events and outings, but she did wish Deanna could have come with her. It didn't matter. For once, she felt like a normal human being, not an animal in a zoo.

As she strolled through the market, the stress of the past several months seemed to evaporate, leaving her with an airiness that was altogether welcome. She couldn't stop the unladylike grin that spread across her face, and she caught a few amused and understanding smiles directed toward her from the people she passed.

She wondered if they could tell the difference between this genuine expression of happiness and the fake, polite one she usually wore when she walked among them on the arm of one of her various suitors. She guessed that some of them could.

She wondered what they thought of her, of her situation. She was their crown princess, and there was no other. If the curse took effect and couldn't be broken, the kingdom would face a devastating decision.

The closest heirs were twins, her second cousins. And they had always been incredibly competitive. Even though the oldest would have the right to the throne, his brother wouldn't give up the position without a fight. No doubt, a civil war would break out when her father died.

The thought seemed to dim the brightness of the day, and Elora quickly shoved it aside. *Do not borrow trouble*, she told herself. That hasn't happened, and it may never happen. And if it does, the council will do everything possible to bring peace. In the meantime, I can only do what I can, and I am.

She expected Jarden to return any day now with the captured elf. He will break the curse, and all will be as it should.

Elora's smile returned at the thought. Thankfully, she still had the capacity to hope. She continued through the market, not looking for anything in particular, just enjoying her freedom.

One booth caught her attention. She gasped when she saw his merchandise and cast an eye over her shoulder at the guards. Had they seen it yet? She didn't think so. They were busy scanning the people on the street.

She hurried over to the booth. "Greetings, young lady. Would you care to take a look at some of our unique offerings?" the man asked.

"Sir," she said frantically, trying to shield his cart from the soldiers behind her. "Do you not know that it is illegal to sell roses in Yeatton?"

"Illegal? To sell such beautiful flowers? Why?"

"You must be a stranger here if you haven't heard about the curse."

"I am a stranger. Are roses cursed in Yeatton?"

"No, but I—the princess is. It is said that she will prick her finger on the thorn of a rose on her eighteenth birthday and fall into an eternal sleep."

"Is today her eighteenth birthday?" the man asked with a raised brow.

"Well, no," Elora admitted with a laugh.

"Then, there can be no harm in my selling them today. Would you like one? It is my gift to you for your warning," he said with an exaggerated bow.

Elora stared at the flowers. They were beautiful, and their scent wafted around her. She breathed in deeply.

She had often seen pictures of them in books. But the pictures did not do them justice. They had always held a unique fascination for her, as most forbidden things will. What could be the harm? As the man said, today wasn't her birthday.

She reached out to take one when a commotion erupted on the far side of the market. A runaway carriage, drawn by wild-eyed horses, careened through the crowd. The guards quickly rushed to her side, their eyes searching the chaos before them for any threats.

Screams filled the air, joined by the cacophony of clattering horse hoofs, stomping feet, and the crash of stalls and carts knocked aside and crushed by the carriage.

Seizing the opportunity, two cloaked figures emerged from the alleyway behind Elora. Her heart quickened as strong arms encircled her. A cloth pressed over her mouth and nose stifled her cries. The world around her spun, and her struggles were in vain as darkness enveloped her consciousness, her guards none the wiser.

When Elora finally awoke, her head pounded. Through bleary eyes, she surveyed her surroundings. The damp air smelled musty, and the sound of her own breathing was the only thing she could hear. She attempted to move her arms, but they were bound tightly.

As her vision cleared, Elora found herself in a dimly lit chamber. The flickering light of a single lantern cast eerie shadows on the walls.

Two cloaked figures stood at a distance. One of them approached, removing the gag from her mouth.

"Welcome back to the land of the living, Your Highness."

Elora's voice trembled with a mix of fear and defiance. "Who are you? What do you want?"

The figure's chilling smile sent shivers down her spine. "We hear you've been trying to capture the mage who cursed you."

Elora swallowed nervously.

"We'd like to ask you some questions about that, if you don't mind," he said with a sneer.

Her heart raced as the gravity of the situation sank in. Maybe her parents had been right. Maybe she should never have tried to take matters into her own hands.

The glare from the campfire caused Jarden's head to throb, the pain blending in with the other aches that plagued him. In fact, his entire body hurt. The failed ambush had cost them dearly—comrades lost, injuries sustained, and their chance to capture the elusive elf slipped through their fingers like sand.

Sitting on a fallen log, Jarden watched the small group of survivors huddled around the campfire.

So few left.

So many lost.

The flickering flames cast eerie shadows on their worn faces, emphasizing the weariness that clung to them. He, himself, was bandaged, and he could hardly move without pain shooting through his body. Their spirits were understandably low. The initial excitement of their mission had given way to bitter disappointment.

The only thing left was to return to Yeatton and face their princess with the news of their failure.

As the men spoke in subdued tones, a rustle of leaves caught Jarden's attention. He reached for his sword but stopped when Adrian emerged from the shadows. Jarden narrowed his eyes, and he exchanged a glance with the others. They had all believed Adrian to be one of the fallen, lost in the chaos of battle. Yet here he was, seemingly unscathed.

Jarden's voice was hoarse as he addressed him. "Adrian. Where have you been?" He gestured for him to come closer, his keen eyes assessing every detail.

Adrian joined the circle, his face a mask of concern as he took in the state of the wounded soldiers. His eyes met Jarden's, and Jarden saw a glimmer of something that didn't sit right with him—a flicker of guilt or unease, perhaps.

Jarden cleared his throat, the effort sending a twinge of pain through his chest. "Where have you been? We thought you were lost in the battle."

Adrian's gaze dropped for a moment before meeting Jarden's again. "I got caught in the fray and must have been knocked out. When I finally came to, it was too late. I couldn't find any of you, and I thought… I thought you were all gone."

Jarden's suspicion deepened. "None of us saw you during the battle. Nor did you warn us when the elves were getting close. Where were you?" Jarden frowned. "You were supposed to be standing watch a mile from our ambush. Did you not see them coming?"

Adrian's gaze wavered, his unease more palpable now. "I'm sorry, Jarden. I never saw them. I heard the sounds of battle behind me and rushed to help."

Jarden's skepticism was marked. "You expect me to believe that? You were supposed to be our lookout. If the elves had advanced, you were to warn us."

Adrian's gaze faltered for a moment before he gained his composure. "I swear, I didn't see them. It's as if they knew where we were and deliberately avoided us."

Jarden's jaw tightened. The possibility that the elves had known about their ambush plan was unsettling. Yet, he couldn't ignore the nagging doubt in the back of his mind.

"By the time I heard the sounds of battle, it was already too chaotic," continued Adrian. "When I tried to get to the fight, I was attacked by one of the elves at the edge. I never made it past him. I was knocked unconscious, and when I woke up, everyone was gone."

Jarden's brows furrowed. "You were knocked unconscious?"

Adrian nodded, his expression almost too composed. "Yes, I woke up later, and I've been trying to find you all ever since."

Jarden's gaze bore into Adrian's eyes, searching for any signs of deceit. "So, you never saw the elves? You didn't notice when they left the road?"

Adrian's eyes remained steady, his tone earnest. "No, Captain, I didn't. By the time I realized something was wrong, it was too late. I swear it."

Jarden's injuries throbbed, but his mind remained sharp. He met Adrian's gaze, a tense silence settling between them.

His instincts screamed that something was amiss, that Adrian's story didn't quite add up. Jarden was a soldier skilled in reading people's expressions and motivations. But he couldn't put his finger on what bothered him, and he couldn't prove anything. He knew he needed to be cautious in how he handled this foreigner. The man's story was plausible, but still...

"Very well, Adrian." His voice held a note of caution. "We've all been through a lot. We need rest. We'll leave for Yeatton in the morning."

Adrian's shoulders seemed to relax slightly, relief and gratitude in his eyes. "Thank you. I'm just glad I found all of you." He smiled around at the group of soldiers. They gazed back at the man who had been a total stranger until a few weeks ago, unsure what to think.

Adrian settled into his bedroll and quickly fell asleep. Jarden's eyes stayed on him long into the night. Something was not right about that man, and he would discover what it was.

Elora squinted her eyes as the door opened. She had been in darkness since her captors left, and the lantern's bright light nearly blinded her. She turned her head away and peered through the narrow slits of her eyes at the man who entered. Her shoulders throbbed from the awkward position they had been in for so long. Her hands, though, were blessedly numb, and she could no longer feel the pain of the ropes cutting into her wrists.

"What is this?" bellowed the newcomer.

The two men who had abducted her hurriedly scrambled in behind him.

"This is no way to treat a lady, let alone a princess. Release her at once."

Without a word, the men rushed over and untied her hands. They pulled her to her feet and gripped her arms tightly. She tried struggling halfheartedly, mainly as a form of protest. There was no way she was getting away from them without help. She would have to bide her time.

"Blindfold her," the man said, and one of the ruffians whipped out a soiled piece of fabric and tied it over her eyes.

"Now, Your Highness, we'll go somewhere more comfortable where you and I can chat. I'm sure you have much to tell me."

Oh, she could think of a few things she'd like to tell him, but now wasn't the time. She needed to know what game he was playing first. "Thank you," she said instead. "It's nice to know that chivalry isn't entirely dead."

The man laughed. "Come, come." She heard his footsteps clipping against the stone floor as he moved out the door. The men kept firm grips on her arms and pulled her out after him.

They traversed several hallways, turning five times. She kept count. They climbed two stairways, twenty-five stairs on the first one and fifty on the second. And they passed through three rooms. She heard the doors open and close as they went.

They could only be in some large estate. No one but the nobility lived in such grandeur. Who, then, was it that held her prisoner? She thought she recognized his voice, but her vision had been so impaired that she couldn't clearly see his face. *But, no*, she thought. It couldn't be someone she knew. They wouldn't dare.

Unless they planned to kill her. That possibility made her stomach clench.

She felt lush carpet under her feet just before the men shoved her onto a soft cushion. They removed the blindfold and backed away. Elora looked around. It was a library, neat and elaborately decorated but small. So, either the estate wasn't as grand as she had thought, or the owner didn't have much interest in books.

Her eyes found the stranger. The man from the market! The man with the roses. That's why his voice sounded familiar. But he had changed his clothes. He was much more finely dressed now. Yes, definitely a gentleman, if not a noble. In title, at least, if not in deed.

"Why have you brought me here?" she asked.

"As my men said. I simply want to have a little chat with you. There is nothing to be afraid of, provided you answer my questions, that is."

Elora tilted her head. "What questions?"

"For one, what do you hope to gain by capturing the elf mage?"

Elora studied him while her mind raced. She didn't want to give in to threats and reveal any information that should be kept secret. But it would be foolish to refuse to divulge harmless information, especially if the result was to be torture of some kind. Was there any way he could use this information against her? She didn't think so.

"I hope to force him to remove the curse."

"And if he cannot do so?"

Elora started. She hadn't thought of that. "He placed the curse on me. He should be able to remove it. All mages can do that."

"Ah," the man said with a grin. "It seems your castle libraries are lacking regarding other species."

"What do you mean?"

"Human mages can undo all of their spells, yes, but that's because their magic doesn't have the power that has been given to the other species. Their magic is borrowed, you might say, from the earth. Elves, however, as well as goblins, have innate magic." He leaned back against the ornate fireplace and crossed his arms. "They are all born with some form of it. It is much more powerful than borrowed magic. And elf mages are those who are born with the ability to control not only their native element but also all other elements and all other magics. They are the most powerful of all."

"What difference does that make? If they are more powerful, they should be more able to break the curse."

"On the contrary. Their magic is so strong that once it is set in place, no one can stop it, not even them. The only way to break a curse is to use the escape route set into the curse upon its casting."

Elora's shoulders slumped, and she fell back against the couch, all royal pride and rebelliousness forgotten in the wake of this information. So, there was no hope then. The curse couldn't be broken unless she fell in love, and she couldn't love. In a few short weeks, her life would be over. Her surroundings faded away as her inner turmoil consumed her. Tears ran down her cheeks, unheeded.

The man stood there, watching her.

"So, you truly didn't know. Interesting."

Elora finally managed to swallow her grief and control her breathing. She glanced up at her abductor through bleary eyes. "Thank you," she said. "Even though that information breaks my heart, it is good to know. Now, we will be better able to prepare for the kingdom's future. I am grateful. Mr..."

"You may call me Lord John."

"Is that your name?"

"No."

"Ah."

Lord John walked over and sat in the chair across from her. "Now, it is your turn. My employer has some questions about your curse."

"Who is your employer."

He wagged his finger at her. "Uh, uh, uh. That would be telling."

She narrowed her eyes. "Okay then. Why does your employer want to know about my curse?"

"Would you believe me if I told you it was so she could help you find a way to break it?"

Elora laughed.

The man smiled at her. "No, I didn't think so. Very well. She wants to know about it because she is interested in duplicating it." He leaned in closely as if sharing a secret. "You see, there is someone she would like to curse, herself." He stood and walked over to the window. "The problem, however, is that she's a normal human, and normal humans don't have access to that kind of power."

"It didn't occur to her to contact a mage?" Elora asked with a sneer.

"Of course," the man turned and studied her. "However, as I'm sure you know, human mages belong to a guild. Guild members must record their magical interactions and any applications for them in the guild records. And the situation she finds herself in is not one that she would like to have recorded. Mages, for some reason, are frustratingly averse to bribery or threats."

He strode back to his chair and sat down again, crossing his legs and picking up the glass on a nearby table. He took a sip of its contents. "That is why she has left the matter in my capable hands."

"I don't know what you expect me to say. I know nothing about the curse except that I'm about to fall victim to it. But even if I did, I wouldn't tell you. Not if you plan to use the information to curse someone else."

"Yes, she thought you might be reluctant. That is why she sent me." He took another sip and watched her over the rim of the glass. "I happen to be an expert at getting information from reluctant people."

"What? Are you going to torture me?" Elora's voice trembled despite her best efforts.

"No, no. Of course not." He sat the glass down and stapled his fingers, tapping them on his lips. He let out a great sigh. "My employer wishes you to remain alive and intact. She wants to observe the progression of your curse, and if I were to mar your features with torture, you certainly wouldn't have any chance of finding true love. No, I have an alternative means of inducing you to comply."

The man waved his hand at the guard standing by the door, and the guard opened it. Two other men walked in, dragging a struggling Rolena. The maid fought against their hold and mumbled into the gag covering her mouth.

Elora jumped to her feet and rushed to them. "If you hurt her, I won't tell you anything!"

The man stood and leaned over the princess, glaring down at her, his face only inches from hers. She instinctively leaned back. "If you don't tell me anything, I will hurt her."

Elora met Roe's gaze. Their eyes wide with panic. What had she gotten her friend into?

Chapter 6

For an instant, concern for her arose inside him. Was she in trouble? What was happening? Panic and helplessness engulfed him before he remembered that he shouldn't care. That he didn't care. She was the enemy.

It was a good thing that she was in danger. Maybe she would die and dissolve the bond early. His torment could finally end. He attempted to ignore the feelings and pay attention to the conference speaker. But they would not be ignored.

The intensity of the emotions grew and ebbed by degrees. What in the world was happening to her? His curiosity was almost as strong as his frustration. Finally, he could take no more. He mentally grabbed the knot of anger and exasperation that had built up inside him and slung it away. *Enough!* he shouted inside his mind. *Be calm!*

The fear suddenly vanished, replaced by surprise. His surprise joined it. What was happening? Why was she shocked at that particular moment?

Had something happened where she was? It would be quite the coincidence. Could she have heard him? No. That wasn't possible. Was it? He couldn't hear her thoughts. How would a mere human be able to hear his?

Curiosity now replaced her surprise. It felt almost like she was reaching out, trying to find something. Had he imbibed his thoughts with magic? He hadn't meant to, but he was so angry. So exasperated. It was possible. Would that have been enough to carry his words across the bond?

This puzzle now consumed all his attention. The lecture was forgotten. His hatred of the girl was forgotten. A discovery like this would be monumental. If it were real.

He decided to experiment. Focusing his magic in his mind, he coated his thoughts with it and sent out a question. *Can you hear me?* Another surge of shock was his only reply. He couldn't hear her response. She had no magic to send back to him.

He decided to try again. *I can't hear your thoughts. I can only feel your emotions. If you can hear me, think of something pleasant that you enjoy, a happy thought.*

For several moments, there was nothing. Had it not worked after all, or did she not have any pleasant memories to draw from? Perhaps her situation did not lend itself to pleasant thoughts.

Finally, he felt it. A surge of happiness. It only lasted a second, but it had unmistakably been there. He jumped up from his seat, said a quick "Excuse me," and rushed out of the room. He needed to find Elion and tell him about this. Imagine, being able to communicate with a human through a bond. The scholars would want to study such a phenomenon.

"What's happening?" asked Roe. "Can you hear anything else?"

"Nothing. It's like it was never there."

"Are you sure you heard it? I mean, it is a little, well, you know."

Elora glared at her friend. "I'm not going crazy. I did hear a voice in my head."

Roe held up her hands. "Okay, okay. I believe you. Who do you think it was?"

Elora shrugged. "I have no idea. Who could do something like that?"

Roe picked up a sandwich off the tray Lord John had sent them and took a bite. They were supposed to be sitting there huddled together, trembling in fear. Roe assumed he expected her to attempt to convince the princess to tell him whatever he wanted to know. They had been afraid at first. They hadn't been able to touch the food he had sent to maintain his façade of hospitality, but now, curiosity overrode that fear.

"You don't think it could be..."

"No, surely not," replied Elora. She didn't need to be told what Roe was thinking. She was thinking the same thing. "How could it be?"

Just then, the door opened, and Lord John walked back in, flanked by his two henchmen. In his hands, he carried a clear glass ball.

He frowned when he didn't find them weeping profusely on each other's shoulders as he had expected. Never mind. They would crumble soon enough if they didn't comply.

"Now," he said, taking the chair across from them and placing the ball on a side table. "First, you should know the rules. This globe," he waved his hand towards the ball, "is enchanted. It is a truth sphere. Its function is simple. As long as the truth is spoken, it will remain clear. However," he held up a finger to emphasize his point. "If a lie is spoken in its presence, the center of the ball will become cloudy and gray."

Elora eyed the item warily.

"If you tell me a lie, or if you refuse to answer any of my questions, my colleagues here," he nodded to the two men behind him, "will be forced to show their displeasure through your friend. Do you understand?"

Elora swallowed and looked at Roe. Their eyes locked for a moment before she turned back to her captor.

"I understand."

"Good. Now, let's begin with something easy. During your research into the elf mage, did you come across any information regarding cursed objects?"

Elora relaxed a little. She felt no compunction answering this one. "Not much," she said. "Just that it was possible. I didn't delve deeper because the topic was unrelated to my situation."

John pursed his lips and leaned back, resting his elbow on the armrests and his chin on his clenched hands. He studied her intently. Elora squirmed in her seat at the scrutiny.

"Very well. What can you tell me about the mage himself? Does he have any weaknesses? Anything that could be used to threaten him? What do you know about his family? His friends?"

"Don't you have spies to gather this information for you?" She crossed her arms defiantly.

"Yes, of course. But infiltrating the elven kingdom takes time. You have been working on this for years, whereas my employer has only recently decided to pursue this avenue. There's no reason we should recreate your efforts when we could ask you about your results."

That sounded logical. Elora gritted her teeth. She didn't want to assist anyone whose desire was to curse someone else. Still, she didn't for a moment believe that the elf would help a human do anything, especially use his spell to curse another innocent.

If he had to suffer for his refusal to do so, it would serve him right for what he did to her. That's the argument she gave herself. However, if she were truly honest, her real motivation stemmed more from not wanting to cause pain or injury to Roe by refusing to answer his question.

"He has no family. His brother was his only remaining family, and he died in the war." She took a deep breath. "He has two close friends: a female mage named Lyariel and a male mage named Edrym. Lyariel is known for her voice. Apparently, her songs can control the elements. It seems that she prefers using fire when fighting. Edrym specializes in lightning and sword fighting. He is said to be an expert swordsman, and he shoots lighting like arrows, but with more accuracy and destruction."

"And Thorn?"

"He is said to use all the elements in battle. It appears that he is equally adept at all of them."

"Hmm." He leaned forward, his elbows on his knees. "Why did you send your men after him now? Why not sooner?"

"He never leaves his city." Elora glanced at the globe. A faint haze began gathering in the center. "As

85

far as I know," she added quickly, and the globe cleared.

John's eyes had also moved to the ball, and he observed its reaction. "Interesting."

"If the ball reacts to all lies like that, why can't you just ask it things? Why did you have to bring me here?" Elora crossed her arms again and glared at the man.

"But it doesn't react to all lies that way. Whatever the speaker believes is true, is taken for truth. This is curious indeed." He studied her again. "Why should it behave differently around you? Tell me this. Have you experienced any side effects from the curse?"

"Side effects? What do you mean?"

"I'll be frank. There is a rumor that the elf who cursed you was bonded to you somehow when the curse was first cast. The rumor said that he is experiencing disturbing effects from it. We have yet to determine their exact nature, though. Perhaps you will be able to answer that question for us."

It took all of Elora's willpower not to glance over at Roe. Could the voice in her head be one of those side effects? Could it really have been the elf who had spoken to her? Whatever it had been, she wasn't quite ready to reveal that bit of information yet. She considered her words carefully.

"From the time the curse landed on me until my kidnapping by your brutes," she said, "I have experienced nothing that I feel could in any way be described as a side effect of the curse."

Lord John's eyes found the globe, and Elora's followed them. Thankfully, it remained clear.

The castle was unusually active when Jarden and his men returned. Alarmingly so. People rushed about in every direction like a hive of agitated bees. It was chaos, a stark contrast to the quiet dignity that usually graced the fortress. Jarden's brow furrowed as he dismounted his horse, the pain in his wounded body temporarily forgotten.

Deanna, Princess Elora's closest friend and confidante, hurried across the courtyard, her chestnut hair flowing behind her like a shimmering waterfall. Jarden quickened his pace to intercept her. He reached out and caught her by the arm. "Deanna, what's going on here? Why is the castle in such disarray?"

Deanna's eyes widened when she saw him, relief crossing her delicate features. "Jarden, you're back. It's terrible. The princess is missing."

Jarden's heart clenched at her words. "Missing? How?"

Deanna glanced around, her voice lowered to a hushed tone. "It happened while you were away. She was in the market, and something—something went wrong. Her guards lost sight of her."

Jarden's mind raced as he processed the information. Could this have anything to do with their failed ambush? He needed to find out more. "Where's the king?"

Deanna pointed toward the castle's grand doors. "He's in the council chambers with his advisors and the officers, trying to figure out what to do."

Without another word, Jarden turned and strode toward the council chambers, his boots echoing in the grand corridor, the heaviness of the news weighing on him. The massive wooden doors swung open, revealing King Leopold seated at the head of a long table. Various officers and advisers surrounded him. The atmosphere was tense, and the urgency in the king's voice was palpable.

Jarden slipped in behind the others. The room was full of military personnel and the king's council, their voices raised as they discussed the princess's disappearance. He had entered the council chamber with all the subtlety of a phantom, choosing a spot at the back of the room, away from the generals who commanded the council's attention.

He was a captain, not as high-ranking as those gathered here, but he knew that the fate of Princess Elora concerned them all. He tried to blend into the background, absorbing every word exchanged.

One of the generals, a grizzled veteran with a stern countenance, cleared his throat. "Your Majesty, we have search parties scouring the nearby areas, and we've sent messengers to surrounding villages and towns. We've also offered a substantial reward for any information that might lead us to Princess Elora.

Scouts have been sent to investigate any leads. But so far, there is no sign of the princess."

The king nodded in acknowledgment. "I want updates on the search every hour. We cannot afford to waste any time."

A scholarly-looking man with spectacles interjected. "Should we dispatch messages to the neighboring kingdoms, asking for their assistance? If anyone has seen or heard anything, it could prove beneficial."

King Leopold considered the suggestion. He didn't like involving the other kingdoms, and the chances of her being taken out of Yeatton were slim. But then again, he didn't want to let his pride stand in the way of getting his daughter back.

"See to it," he told the man.

Another advisor, a wiry man with a keen eye, leaned forward. "Your Majesty, should we consider the possibility of foul play within the castle? Perhaps someone close to the princess is involved."

King Leopold's eyes darkened at the suggestion, but he knew no avenue could be left unexplored. "Yes, yes, you're right. We must consider all possibilities. Investigate anyone who had regular access to her."

Jarden watched as the discussions continued, options and strategies presented. They discussed questioning known troublemakers and spies within the kingdom. They discussed increasing patrols and inspections at the city gates. They discussed the law concerning searching people's homes. Everything was considered.

Jarden noted their diligence, but a gnawing feeling of unease settled in his gut. He couldn't help but wonder if this had to do with their failed ambush. Thorn could have magicked himself to the castle. He'd been here before. What if he had taken her back to Allanar in revenge for their attack?

As the meeting came to an end, Jarden quietly left the council room. They had the main avenues of investigation covered. But he didn't believe they would find her that way. He would have to do some investigating of his own.

Adrian was waiting for him when he left the castle, leaning against a stone wall, his expression curious and concerned. He had overheard Deanna mention the princess's disappearance and had been waiting for Jarden to return with information.

"What do they know, Captain? Do they have any suspects? Were there any witnesses?"

Jarden regarded him with wariness. "No witnesses thus far. And as for suspects..." He trailed off, a shadow of concern crossing his face.

Adrian's eyes gleamed with a strange intensity. "Jarden, we need to find her. I can help. Just tell me what to do."

Jarden studied Adrian for a moment, his instincts telling him that there was more to the man than met the eye. "I'll keep you informed, Adrian. For now, stay vigilant."

As Jarden walked away, Adrian's eyes shot around the courtyard, taking in the scene. Everyone appeared to be focused on their own tasks. No one seemed to pay any particular attention to him. Satisfied, he turned and hurried out the gate into town. He had someone he needed to meet.

"Is that all you can tell me of the elf and the curse?"

"Yes," answered Elora wearily. "I don't know anything else." The interrogation seemed to have gone on forever. She didn't have answers to most of the questions, and regarding the others, she didn't see how her responses could benefit anyone. So, she told him what she knew. Thankfully, they hadn't done anything to Roe yet.

"Let's move on to a different topic then, shall we," said Lord John. He walked to the fireplace, then turned and headed back to the door. "If you do succumb to the curse," he said, "which seems quite likely, what will happen to the succession of the throne?"

The princess hesitated. Why was he asking this? "This has nothing to do with the elf or his magic. Why do you want to know?"

"I will hide nothing from you, Your Highness," he said with a bow. "The answer is quite simple. Without its crown princess, there's a great possibility that the kingdom of Yeatton will be thrown into a civil war. Chaos in a country always weakens it. Such a situation would make your country ripe for an enterprising individual to come in and take over."

Elora's right hand flew to her heart, and her other grasped Roe's tightly. "I will not help you with that, sir."

He stopped his pacing and pulled a pipe from his jacket pocket. He took a moment to light it and stuck it in his mouth. Taking a puff, he tried to stare her down.

"Do what you will to me, My Lord; I am ready to die for my kingdom. You'll get nothing out of us," said Roe bravely.

John glanced at one of the men standing behind him, and the man walked over and struck Roe across the cheek. Elora cried out and pulled her friend to her, shielding her body with her own. "Stop it!" she yelled. "I won't betray my kingdom, and hurting this innocent woman isn't going to change that. Just let her go."

John motioned to the man, and he raised his hand again. Before he could repeat his strike, a loud pounding came from the door. The man looked back at Lord John, and he held up his hand for him to wait. The other man opened the door, and a little girl walked in with a note. She quickly handed it to the nobleman and scurried out.

John scanned the paper, folded it, and stuck it in his pocket. "It seems providence has granted you a reprieve," he said. "I will return shortly to resume our conversation. I encourage you to strongly consider the consequences of continued defiance."

Lord John and the two men left the room, locking the door behind them. Elora turned to Roe.

"Are you hurt?"

"Not much, Your Highness. It just stings a little. I'm sure it'll be fine in no time."

Elora wasn't convinced. The whole side of her face shone a bright red.

"I'm so sorry," she hugged her friend tightly. "This is all my fault."

Roe hugged her back. "Of course it's not, Princess. You didn't ask those men to kidnap you." She pulled away and stared Elora in the eyes. "Did you?" she asked with mock sternness.

Elora laughed. "No, I did not."

"There, then. See, it's not your fault."

Elora gave her another quick hug and jumped up from the couch. "Since providence has given us a reprieve, we shouldn't waste it. Let's see if we can find some way out of here."

They wandered around the room, examining everything closely. One glance told them that the only apparent exits were the single door and window. The men had locked the door, and the window was three stories high. But Elora's castle was full of secret passageways. Why shouldn't this house have some?

So, they looked.

Everywhere.

Just when they were about to see if they could climb out the window and scale down the wall, they heard a key being turned in the lock. They rushed back to the couch and sat down. The sound continued.

"Why's it taking them so long to unlock the door?" whispered Roe.

Elora shrugged. "Maybe the key got bent."

Finally, the door opened, and a man stepped in.

"Adrian?" Elora didn't know what to think. "What are you doing here?"

"I'm here to rescue you," he said with a grin. He held up a bundle of thin, keylike pieces of metal. "It's good I learned how to pick locks back in Penningdon."

"Yes," laughed Elora.

"Come. We need to hurry. They could return at any time." He held out his hand, and Elora hurried to take it.

"How did you find us?" They had reached one of the staircases she remembered. Adrian peeked around the wall to ensure no one was in sight before they descended.

"I told you. I have contacts," he replied with a sly smile. "One of them saw you being taken. He recognized you but was too scared to go to the king. He thought he might be accused of playing some role in your abduction. Apparently, he hadn't heard about the reward yet." Adrian laughed.

Elora glanced at him as they reached the bottom of the stairs and hurried down the corridor. Did he only rescue her for the reward?

"And your mission?" she whispered. "Was it successful?"

"Alas, no. We were defeated quite soundly. Jarden is alright," he said quickly, noticing the concern in her eyes. "Though he was injured. But we lost many of the men."

"What happened?"

"I promise I'll tell you all about it later. We need to get out of here first."

"Of course," Elora said, feeling justifiably chastised. He squeezed her hand to lessen the sting of his words and didn't let go. Elora felt a blush steal up her face as they quietly made their way through the house.

"Mother, please," Elora implored, her voice soft yet unwavering. "Just this one night. If we must have a ball, why don't we have one without any men? Can't you imagine it? What fun it will be!"

Queen Callista's regal countenance registered her shock. "No men, Elora? That's simply unheard of. Balls are a time for you to meet potential suitors, to socialize, to—"

"To be scrutinized and paraded like a prized mare," Elora finished, her tone tinged with weariness. "Mother, I've tried, truly, I have. But I'm tired. Tired of the endless stream of suitors, the polite smiles, the same conversations. I want just one evening to enjoy the company of my friends without the weight of expectations."

The queen regarded her daughter, torn between tradition and a mother's desire to see her child happy. Elora's plea was not without merit, and Callista knew the weight the curse was on her daughter.

Elora took a step closer, her gaze filled with earnestness. "I promise, Mother, it's just one night. Tomorrow, I'll be back to the business of courtship, but tonight, can't I have this reprieve? Please. As a reward for surviving my capture and returning to you safely." That was a low blow, and she knew it, but she didn't care.

The queen let out a sigh, her resistance waning. "Very well, Elora. One night, without men. But you must promise me you'll resume searching for a suitable match afterward."

Elora's face lit up with a grateful smile. "Thank you, Mother. I promise. Tomorrow, I'll return to my duty with renewed determination. But tonight, we'll have a ball to remember."

With a nod of reluctant agreement, Queen Callista conceded. "I don't know what your father will say about this," she mumbled as she left the room.

Elora let out a most unladylike squeal and rushed out to find Deanna.

The king had wasted no time in sending soldiers to the manor, which sat in the countryside to the south of the city walls. Unfortunately, the place was deserted. Though, the captain of the guard did know the house. It was the home of the Duke of Barton. He had been overseas visiting his daughter and her new husband in the Kingdom of Gilwater for the past year.

Clearly, someone had taken advantage of his absence. New investigations would follow. But for tonight, she would put all thoughts of that out of her mind. Her father had the situation under control, and she trusted him to see it through. Tonight, she would dance.

Chapter 7

The castle's grand ballroom shimmered with opulence and elegance, its crystal chandeliers casting a soft, warm glow over the assembled guests. Princess Elora stood at the top of the staircase, her heart fluttering with anticipation as she looked down upon the dazzling spectacle below.

Tonight's ball was a celebration, a triumphant return after her harrowing ordeal, and the atmosphere was charged with excitement. The kingdom had never seen such a ball as this.

Elora descended the staircase gracefully in her resplendent gown, a vision of regal beauty. Her arrival drew the guests' attention, and the room fell into a hushed silence.

"Welcome, everyone, to my celebration ball!" Princess Elora's voice echoed off the walls. The ladies in attendance glanced around the room curiously while applauding politely.

Elora smiled at their confusion. "You may notice that this ball is a bit different than the others we have been having. If you look around, you will see that there is something missing, or rather, a few someones missing."

Scattered laughter floated up to her. "Where are all the men?" cried a voice from the crowd.

Elora grinned. "Not here. And they won't be tonight." Surprised gasps and murmurs erupted around the room.

"Tonight is just for us. No men. No competition. No pretending. No pressure. Tonight, we can just be ourselves. We can eat as much junk food as we want. We can talk freely, laugh freely, and act freely. The guards have strict orders to keep all men away. So ladies, let's enjoy our freedom!"

Shouts, laughter, and applause erupted from the girls. And the all-female orchestra burst into song. There would be no waltzes that night, only fun, energetic music. And the audience appreciated the change. Girls grabbed the arms of their friends and ran to the dance floor, swinging each other around and reveling in the hilarity.

Some of the more reserved ladies of the court stood on the outskirts and watched, but even they enjoyed the fun of it all. The atmosphere was charged like never before, and the guards standing outside chuckled at the sounds emanating through the doors, some wishing they could join them and others thankful they could not.

Deanna and Roe rushed over to Elora as she made her way to the dessert tables. Roe had helped Elora dress before she slipped on her borrowed gown, having been given special permission to attend the party. But Deanna had not seen her friend since she returned to the castle. The queen and king had grabbed her and whisked her away as soon as she entered the doors.

"Tell me all about it," she said, grabbing each girl by the arm.

"Later," whispered Elora as one of her mother's friends approached the group. "In my room after the ball." Deanna reluctantly released them and turned to greet the lady. It seemed everyone wanted to talk to Elora that night. After about an hour, the older ladies took their leave. There was no need for chaperones without men in attendance, so they felt no obligation to stay any longer. The guards would keep the ladies safe. Some of the younger girls reluctantly left with them, but a large group remained.

As the evening unfolded, Elora danced and mingled with her closest friends, a group of young women who had been eagerly awaiting her return. They formed a circle on the dance floor, laughing and twirling together, the absence of the men unnoticed amid their camaraderie.

"Elora, were you not frightened?" one of the girls asked, concern etching her features as she caught her breath between dances.

Elora paused momentarily, her thoughts drifting back to the dark room where she had first been held captive. "I was scared," she admitted softly, "but I knew I had to stay strong."

Another girl chimed in, her voice filled with subdued excitement. "And who rescued you, Elora? It must have been a valiant knight!"

Elora's cheeks flushed as she thought of Adrian. "It was Adrian," she replied, her voice tinged with gratitude. "He came to my rescue."

Excited whispers rippled through the group of girls, their eyes wide with curiosity. "Adrian?" one of them repeated, her tone filled with fascination. "Who's he? What's he like?"

Elora chuckled at their eagerness. "He's brave, resourceful, and a skilled warrior," she answered. "But he's also very modest. He didn't take any credit for finding me. He just told father that he got lucky. But that's not true."

One of her friends squealed as she clasped her hands and bounced up and down. "Elora, it sounds like you're in love! Do you love him?"

Elora blushed. "I don't know him that well yet. I just admire him. He seems to be a good guy."

"Is he handsome?" another girl asked with a wink as she leaned in closely.

"Shut up," said Elora, pushing her away.

"Well, is he?" persisted the girl.

"Alright, yes. He's very handsome."

"Ohhh," said several of them in unison.

The girls erupted into giggles, and the questions kept coming. They were enamored with the hero who had saved their princess, and their curiosity about him seemed boundless.

As the evening wore on, the ball continued in a whirl of music and laughter late into the night.

"And this Adrian rescued you?" asked Deanna when the girls were finally alone and could talk freely. "Why have I never heard of him?"

Elora stood by the window gazing out into the night. Should she tell them? There was no one she trusted more, but... She sighed. "Promise you won't get mad."

Deanna squinted her eyes and tilted her head. "Why would I get mad?"

"Because," said Elora, coming over to sit on the bed between Deanna and Roe. "I've been keeping a secret from you."

Deanna's brows came together in a most forceful way. She huffed, crossed her arms, and leaned back against the headboard. "I thought we told each other everything. I certainly have no secrets from you."

"It was for your protection. Please understand," pleaded the princess. "I thought—no—I knew that if I told you, you would want to get involved, and it might be dangerous. It was, as it turned out."

"Well, what is it?" asked Deanna, clearly not mollified.

"I've been investigating the elf who cursed me. I thought if I could capture him somehow, I might be able to force him to break the curse."

"Elora! He's a powerful mage. If he finds out, there's no telling what he might do."

"He's already cursed me. What else could he do?"

"He could come after your family?" suggested Roe timidly.

"But why? I'm the one after him. He would have no reason to punish them."

"Unless he knew that would hurt you," suggested Deanna.

Elora groaned and dropped her face into her hands. "I didn't think about that."

Deanna rubbed her friend's back soothingly. "I know you had our best interests in mind, but I wish you would have told us."

"What I don't understand," said Roe, "is how you did this by yourself and how in the world you expected to capture him."

"Well, I didn't actually do it by myself. I had a little help."

"From this Adrian?" asked Deanna, her eyes once again brightening with curiosity.

"This last time."

"And before him?" asked Roe.

Elora grinned and elbowed Deanna teasingly. "Jarden has been helping me."

Deanna giggled. "So, that's why he's been spending so much time talking to you. Hmm. Maybe he really doesn't like you after all." She tapped her finger against her lips and stared off into the distance.

"Sooo," cut in Roe, "Who's this Adrian that rescued us?"

"I don't know much about him," said Elora. "I met him in my private garden late one night."

"Oh?" said Deanna, eyes wide. She had their attention now.

"Not like that." Elora glowered at her friends. "I was actually meeting Jarden."

Deanna put her hands on her hips. "I don't think I like you meeting my man in your private garden in the middle of the night."

Roe snorted, but Elora ignored the interruption.

"He had just returned from a mission across the mountains and had gone by Allanar to see the elven spy helping us."

"Why would an elf betray one of his own people to the humans?" asked Roe.

"I don't know," admitted Elora. "Maybe he has a personal grudge against the mage."

"Do you trust him?" Deanna leaned back on the bed and rested her head on her hands.

"I don't know him," replied Elora, "but I trust Jarden, and Jarden trusts him."

"Then he must be okay," said Deanna with a nod.

"I want to know," said Roe, "where Adrian comes into the picture."

"After I met Jarden, I waited a few minutes in the garden to think and let him get past the guards. Then." She lowered her voice mysteriously. "I heard a noise in the bushes, and this man walked out."

Deanna gasped and covered her mouth in mock horror. "You must have been terrified."

Elora chuckled at her friend's antics. "A little frightened, I'll admit. He had followed Jarden here from Allanar."

"Wait a minute," said Deanna, sitting up abruptly. "I don't know if I believe that. Jarden would know if someone followed him."

"That's what I thought, and I said as much to the man, but he said he had some magic or ability or something that helped him do it."

"Do you believe him?" asked Roe.

Elora shrugged. "I don't have any reason not to. He couldn't have followed Jarden otherwise, and how would he know we were meeting there if he didn't?"

"I guess it makes sense," Roe admitted reluctantly.

"I don't suppose he told you what his magic was?" asked Deanna.

"No," Elora scoffed. "He said we didn't know each other well enough for the sharing of such secrets."

Roe picked up a pillow and hugged it. "That seems smart."

"I guess." Elora scooted back from the edge, put her feet on the bed, and hugged her knees. "The important thing is...promise you won't tell anyone."

The girls' eyes went wide. "We promise," they said in unison.

"I really like him."

"Really?" squealed Deanna.

"Like, love like?" asked Roe.

"Not quite love like, yet, but like like. In fact, he's the first person I've ever really liked."

"Do you think he could be the one to break the curse?" asked Roe.

"I don't know, but I do want to get to know him better. I still have a few weeks." She smiled. "Maybe something will grow there."

"And that elf thought he could keep you from loving." Roe hugged her pillow tighter.

"I wish the mage could see you with this Adrian," said Deanna with a huff. "He'll see he can't keep a princess of Yeatton down."

"Oh!" said Roe and Elora at the same time. The girls glanced at each other and burst out laughing. Deanna watched them quizzically.

"We forgot to tell you," said Elora.

"Tell me what?"

"When we were captured, Elora discovered something about the mage. Tell her."

"First, one of the questions that the man asked me was whether I had experienced any side effects from the curse. I didn't know what he meant at the time, but he said there was a rumor that the elf mage was bonded to me somehow when he cursed me."

"Bonded to you? What does that mean?"

"I don't know, for sure, but..." Elora glanced at Roe. "I heard his voice in my head."

Deanna shifted onto her knees and grabbed Elora by the shoulders. "What do you mean you heard his voice in your head."

Elora laughed. "I heard his voice in my head."

"Oh. Wow! What did he say?"

"First, he said 'enough' or 'stop' or something like that. Then, 'be calm.' After that, he asked if I could hear him. He sounded surprised. I mean, as much as a mysterious voice in your head can sound surprised."

"Do you really think it was him?"

"I don't know who else it could be. I don't normally have men talking to me in my mind. And the man did say that he'd heard the elf was experiencing some side effect."

"Don't forget," said Roe, "He also told you he could feel your emotions but couldn't hear your thoughts."

"Yes, that's right."

"If he can talk to you like that, why has he not done so before," asked Roe.

The girls sat in silence, each trying to think of an answer.

"What was it that he said," asked Deanna.

"I think it was 'enough.'"

"That's it then," said Deanna. "If he can feel your emotions, I assume you were feeling some pretty strong ones then."

"I most certainly was."

"Perhaps they were getting on his nerves."

"What do you mean?" asked Roe.

"Well, it must be difficult to concentrate on anything with someone else's emotions constantly in your head. With you being kidnapped and scared. Maybe he'd had enough of it."

"You're right," said Elora with a mischievous glint in her eye. "It must be quite annoying."

"What are you thinking?" asked Roe.

"I'm thinking it's high time I paid back that pesky elf for what he did to me. I might not be able to kidnap him, but if I can annoy the fire out of him, that would be satisfying to a small degree."

Roe sat up straighter. "How will you know if it works?"

"I'll see if I can get him to say something again. He sounded quite exasperated the last time."

"If he's been feeling your emotions the whole time, though, and only now spoke, he must be an incredibly patient man. You'll have to get him worked up," Roe said.

A huge smile spread across Elora's face. "I think I can do that."

"So." Deanna lay back on the bed. "What shall we start with?"

"How about love?" suggested Roe. "He said he's prevented you from loving. If you filled his mind with that emotion, it would be just what he deserves. He doesn't have to know if it's a different kind of love."

"I like that," said Deanna. "It will keep him guessing. He'll wonder if you've found some way around the curse. Maybe he'll even come to check, and you can capture him then."

"That would be nice," said Elora. "Even if I can't force him to break the curse, I could make his life miserable. Alright then, give me ideas. What can I think about that will make me feel love?"

The girls spent the next hour provoking emotions in Elora, and she felt each one as deeply and as vigorously as she was able, yet no voice responded. They were having too much fun to be terribly disappointed, though, and decided to try again the next day. Elora went to sleep that night feeling happier and calmer than she had in years.

"She knows," said Thorn, his head falling into his hand.

"Who knows what?" asked Edrym.

"The princess. She knows I can feel her emotions, and she's been plaguing me with emotion after emotion all day."

"How does she know that?"

Thorn told him about speaking to her.

"Does father know?"

"Yes, I told him and some of the scholars at the conference. They wanted to study me, of course."

Edrym guffawed. "And what did you say to that."

Thorn glared at him. "What do you think I said?"

"I can only imagine. I'm sure they were very disappointed."

"Yes," Thorn replied dryly. "They'll get over it."

They sat in the mage guild's workroom, crushing and bottling dried herbs. Typically, this was a job for the novices, but Thorn enjoyed it. He found the repetitive task calming, especially amidst the recent turmoil in his mind.

"Ugh!" He gripped his head again and laid his forehead on the table. "She's at it again."

"More so than usual?" Edrym was beginning to get a little concerned. "Should I find Father?"

"No, no." Thorn waved his hand dismissively and slowly raised his head. "I can handle it. Though, she does appear quite determined to torment me. It's as if she's feeling every emotion with her utmost strength. It's like—like she's shouting them at me."

Edrym pulled the stopper from a vial and set it aside. "You can hardly blame her."

Thorn gazed at his friend incredulously. "You're taking her side now?"

Edrym laughed. "Of course not. But you must admit, she is innocent in this."

"You've been hanging around Lyariel too much," Thorn mumbled.

Edrym held up a finger to stop his protest. "It is her parents you wanted to punish, not her. And this is the only way she can get any sort of revenge. Surely, you can't deny her this small pleasure."

"This small pleasure, as you call it, will drive me insane if it doesn't stop." He winched as another strong emotion came through the bond.

"Maybe you should talk to her again."

"I'm afraid that's what she wants."

"Well, give it to her. In fact," said Edrym with a sly grin, "why don't you give her a taste of her own medicine."

Thorn's brows rose with interest. "What do you mean?"

"She's plaguing you with her emotions. Why don't you plague her with your thoughts. Talk to her.

Constantly. Drive her as crazy as she's driving you. That should make her stop."

Thorn let out a roar of laughter. "I love that idea." He tapped the bottle he was working with against the table. "But what should I say? I've never been verbose. I don't know that I could carry on a one-sided conversation long enough to drive anyone crazy."

Edrym turned to the bookshelves behind them and pursued the shelves. Finally, he pulled out a thick tome. "Here, you could do with a refresher on magic herbology. You should read this to her. It might do you both some good."

A wicked smile spread across his face as he took the book from his friend.

Elora sat at the head table in the dining room with the Duke of Waldover on her left and Adrian on her right. It had taken a bit of convincing since he didn't have a title, but the queen had finally agreed to allow the man to attend. It was no secret that the princess was interested in him, and any love was better than no love.

The Duke of Waldover was an older gentleman and already married, so he wouldn't bother them. Elora was looking forward to the evening in Adrain's company. Cautiously, she allowed herself to hope again.

Deanna watched them from her seat on the other side of the table, practically ignoring the young man beside her who was making every attempt to get her attention. He finally sighed and turned to the lady on his left, leaving Deanna free to observe their interaction.

109

She was attempting to be subtle, but subtility had never been her strong suit. Elora tried to ignore her nosy friend and soon became so engrossed in her conversation that she was quite easily able to do so.

Adrian described to her his travels. He described the vast cave networks he encountered in the Kingdom of Dramnott and the gem-studded caves of Kelgrod. He talked of a journey to Gilwater and the merpeople he had seen there. Elora found it all fascinating until he suddenly switched gears and began reciting the herbs needed to make a potion to cure diarrhea. She wrinkled her nose in distaste. They were eating, for goodness sake.

"I'm sorry. What did you say?" she asked.

"The magic of the merpeople is in their voices. Their songs are so beautiful, it's said some of them can cause you to die of a broken heart."

"Oh. Wow!" she said, baffled.

Adrian continued. But the voice she had heard before returned. This time it spoke of the soil type and consistency required to grow nightlinde herbs. She glanced at Deanna, confusion written across her face, until she understood. Her eyes cleared, and her whole face shone. Adrian continued talking, not noticing her distraction.

Deanna watched her. "What?" she mouthed across the table.

"It's him," Elora mouthed back.

Deanna shook her head, not understanding.

Elora pointed to her head, attempting to make the motion seem casual to any others who might see. Then she moved her fingers in a speaking motion. "He's talking to me," she mouthed.

110

Deanna's eyes widened. "What's he saying?"

Elora held up her finger and turned to Adrian. She listened for a moment to catch up to the flow of the conversation she had missed in her distraction.

"That is all fascinating. I have long held an interest in other cultures. Please, don't lose your train of thought. I want to hear more, but I must ask you to excuse me for a moment."

He seemed disappointed at the interruption but stood, as any gentleman would when she rose and left the table. She walked out into the hall and waited. She didn't have to wait long before Deanna joined her.

The girl grabbed Elora's arms and bounced on her feet. "He finally said something?"

"He's still saying something." Elora laughed. "I must have annoyed him more than I realized."

"What do you mean?"

"He's lecturing me on magical herbs."

Deanna paused for a moment to take in the significance of that information. Then burst out laughing. "He's paying you back!"

Elora nodded with a grin.

"You must have really gotten to him."

"If he thinks he can defeat me this easily, he's got another think coming."

"I have faith in you. You can out-annoy anyone."

"I don't know whether that's a compliment or an insult."

"Take it as you will," Deanna said with a smirk. "Now, you better get back in there. You have a real man waiting for you. Let that old elf feel some of the emotions Adrian raises. Unless..." she winked at the princess. "They are too private." With that, she returned to the dining hall.

"Oh!" cried Elora as her friend walked away. She felt heat rush into her cheeks. What did she feel for Adrian? He was certainly attractive, and she found his conversation interesting. Was that enough? Could that be love?

As a description of temperate zones and their importance in magic herb root systems streamed through her mind, Elora marched back to the table.

Chapter 8

A *hh! Shut up!* Princess Elora had finally had enough. With all of her bravado to Deanna, she couldn't deny that she was losing this battle.

When silence met her outburst, she froze and held her breath. *Can you hear me?* she finally thought. Nothing. After days of their mental and emotional skirmish, her mind felt strangely empty, bereft somehow. Pleasantly so, for the most part, but there, sitting in her room at night, the darkness all around her, loneliness descended over her and reawakened her despair.

She hadn't realized it until that moment, but the small battle she had been engaged in with the elf had proven a good distraction from her plight. She quickly tempered the negative emotions as she had grown so adept at doing over the last several weeks. She certainly didn't want him to feel her sorrow at the absence of his voice.

The mage never did reply, and she finally got a good night's sleep, void of the abnormal dreams of herbs, mystical animals, or elven history she had been having as the sound of his voice invaded her subconscious throughout the night.

The next morning, the voice was still silent. She couldn't get the possibilities out of her mind as Roe helped her prepare for the day.

"I think I spoke to the elf last night."

Roe's hand froze, the brush halfway through a stroke. "What happened?" she asked as she resumed brushing her hair.

"The constant talking," Elora said, watching the maid through the mirror, "it finally got to me. I told him to shut up. And he did."

Roe laughed. "You told him to shut up? Did he say anything to you?"

"Not a word. And he still hasn't."

"He's stopped talking to you before," Roe said. "Maybe he's just off doing something else."

"Perhaps, I mean, he can't sit around and read to me all the time. He must have other things he needs to attend to. And you're right. There have been occasional intermissions in his speeches. But this time feels different. The timing was so perfect. I told him to be quiet, and he immediately did. It would be a strange coincidence."

Just then, a knock sounded on the door, and Deanna burst in, followed by a maid carrying a breakfast tray.

"My apologies, Your Highness," the maid said, setting the tray on the table. "There is no fruit this morning."

Elora turned to her, bewildered. "No fruit? But there's always fruit. What's happened?"

The maid bobbed a curtsey. "Food has been disappearing from the kitchens," she said. "Cook is beside herself. This morning, when we came in, there was more missing than usual. And all the fruit."

The three friends glanced at each other, surprise evident on all their faces.

"Things have certainly not gotten dull around here lately," said Deanna with a chuckle.

"Thank you, Maria. That will be all." The maid curtsied and left. Roe nudged Elora to her feet and went to the closet for a gown.

"Wait till you hear what else has happened," she told Deanna from inside the closet.

"Ohh. What? Tell me." Deanna plopped down at the table and began nibbling on a biscuit.

Elora shared her suspicions about the elf being able to hear her. "And," she added as Roe slipped the gown over her head. "I think there might be more. I'm feeling a little angry right now."

"Why?" asked Deanna.

"That's just it. There's no reason. In fact, I'm quite happy at the moment."

"But you said you were angry." Roe crossed her arms and looked quizzically at the princess.

"No," Elora corrected, holding up a hand. "I said, 'I'm feeling angry.'"

Roe and Deanna glanced at each other in confusion until Deanna understood. She squealed and bounced in her seat. "You can feel his emotions!"

Elora nodded. "I think so."

Roe's eyes went wide. "What does that mean?" she asked.

"Maybe," suggested Deanna excitedly, "Maybe, since the curse is getting so close, the bond that the kidnapper talked about is getting stronger."

At the reminder of the curse, all Elora's enthusiasm fled. She only had about a week left before it took

115

effect. If things didn't progress faster with Adrian, she was as good as dead.

Adrian stood in his room in the barracks, staring into a hand mirror, waiting, his mind a confusion of thoughts and emotions. His mission had seemed so simple when he had begun: gain the trust of the princess and discover whatever you can about the curse. Also, gain the confidence of the elf mage if possible and learn what you can from him.

Adrian had known that Elora was attempting to capture the elf, so there wouldn't be any problem interacting with both of them. Nothing could be easier for an elite spy from Penningdon, the kingdom where subterfuge was practically required to survive, at least in the court.

He had accomplished his mission, at least the initial stages of it. Both the princess and the mage trusted him. He had been able to sneak in questions about the curse throughout his conversations with Elora, and he believed he now knew everything she did, especially when he combined his information with that gathered by Count Reginald and the men they had hired to kidnap her.

His timely rescue of her had erased all doubt from her mind, and she had been most forthcoming.

Now, he should move on to the elf. The mage owed him a favor. He simply needed to find him and call in that favor. He would get what he needed from him, then return to his employer and live in luxury on the large reward she had promised.

There was no reason for him to stay any longer in Yeatton; however, he found himself surprisingly reluctant to leave. With only about a week left until Elora's birthday, he realized he wanted to be here for her. They had been spending a great deal of time together lately, and he had grown quite fond of the beautiful princess. He believed that she shared his feelings.

It might even be possible for him to break the curse for her. He had no doubt that his employer would find that information valuable, as well, even though she would undoubtedly consider his feelings for the princess a betrayal of his mission. She might even lose faith in him and his report. No, he wouldn't tell her that. He knew his employer well. She had attempted to kill her own stepdaughter and would have if the huntsman hadn't betrayed her. A woman like that wouldn't hesitate to kill a spy.

But still, he knew she would order him to go find the elf unless he had some good reason not to, and he wanted to stay. He felt a stubborn resolve rise in him at the thought. He wanted to stay. If he could break Elora's curse, there would be no reason for him to return to Pennigdon. He could stay here and be a king someday.

The mirror fogged up, gray smoke swirling in its depths. Adrian took a deep breath and schooled his features.

"Report," said a voice as the face of a beautiful woman appeared in the mirror.

Adrian bowed. "I have sent the letter containing the information via homing pigeon. You should receive it soon." He hesitated. "There doesn't seem to be any more information I can get from the princess about the curse. I believe she has told me all she knows."

"Then head across the mountains. See what you can discover from the mage. Also, see if you can get him to give you a cursed object. That will be the easiest way of administering it. Barring that, try to get the actual wording of the curse itself. Perhaps our mages can do something with it."

"Your Majesty," Adrian interjected before the queen could dismiss him. "I was thinking that I might stay here until the curse falls. While I don't think the princess knows anymore, there still might be something we can learn from watching the curse take effect. Also, it is possible that someone could break it. With your permission, I would like to be on hand to witness this." He bowed again.

The queen studied him through the enchanted glass.

"It should only delay me a few days," he said when she remained silent.

"Very well," she answered, suspicion evident in her tone. "But no more than a day after the curse takes hold. If anyone is to awaken her, they will most likely do so immediately. I don't have the time to waste sitting around waiting.

In the meantime, go to the village of Greenbrier. It is only a few days' ride from there. Find a mage named Berrymore. He is considered an expert in enchanted objects. Discover his abilities. Specifically, find out if he can imbue something with an elven curse. I've heard he is a little friendlier to his wealthy friends than the mages here in Penningdon. We may be able to make use of his services later.

"Yes, Your Majesty," Adrian said with a bow. The figure in the mirror faded away, and the man was left staring at his reflection. He gritted his teeth in frustration.

He didn't dare disobey the queen, but he wanted these last few days with Elora. He needed them. He didn't know how strong her feelings were for him yet. With a huff, he stuffed the mirror back into his bag and slung the door to his room open. There, standing in the hallway, was Jarden. A scowl adorned his face.

"Who were you talking to?"

Adrian panicked but managed to keep the emotion from showing. "I was just talking to myself," he said with a laugh. "I do that sometimes. It helps me think."

Jarden narrowed his eyes and glared at the man. *What had he heard?* thought Adrian.

"If you'll excuse me, I'll get some training in before lunch." Adrian eased around the captain and headed to the training field, using all of his control not to look back.

Deanna flounced into the orchard, eyes bright and face glowing. She wound through the shadows of the trees, grabbing an apple off a low-hanging limb as she passed. Up ahead, she saw him, a figure standing at the edge of the grove with his back to her. He turned at the sound of her approach.

"You wanted to see me, Captain Jarden?" She didn't even attempt to hide the pleasure in her voice.

"What does Elora feel for Adrian?"

119

Deanna's spirits fell crashing down around her feet. So, he did like Elora. And he was jealous? At that moment, she felt a twinge of jealousy herself, but she quickly pushed it aside. Elora was her friend. She wouldn't let a man come between them.

"Why do you ask?" She stared at her fingernails while she waited for his reply.

"I don't trust him," he said fiercely. "I heard him talking to someone in his room this morning, but when I questioned him about it, he said he was talking to himself." Jarden ran his hand through his short black hair.

"Who do you think it was?"

"I don't know, but this isn't the first time he's acted suspiciously. I still have questions about his actions during our ambush attempt, too."

"So, you're not jealous?"

"Jealous?" Jarden repeated with surprise. "Why would I be jealous? The man could be a spy come to sabotage us."

A grin spread across Deanna's face.

"I don't dare say anything to anyone about it, though, because if the princess likes him, he could be the one to break the spell. I wouldn't want to do anything to prevent that. He seems to be the only one she cares for. The question is," he continued, "how much does she like him? Is it love?"

Deanna pursed her lips in thought. She sighed. "I don't think so. She finds him handsome, and she enjoys his company, but..."

"But what?"

"I don't know. I can't put my finger on it exactly. Her eyes don't light up when she talks about him. She gets more excited when she talks about the elf," Deanna added with a chuckle. Then, as she realized what she'd said, she covered her mouth with her hand, her eyes wide.

Jarden frowned. "Why does she talk about the elf?"

Deanna just stared at him, her mouth closed tightly.

"Deanna," he said, grabbing her shoulders. "Why does the princess talk about the elf?"

Deanna stared into his deep brown eyes. Her resistance broke down, and she told him everything: the questions the kidnapper had asked, the voice in her head, her feeling strange emotions, everything. She felt a pang of guilt when she was done, but she didn't think the princess would mind Jarden knowing. She hoped she wouldn't mind.

"I have heard of such things, at least similar things, from my contacts in the elven kingdom."

"You mean it's normal for them to hear each other's thoughts?"

"No, not exactly normal, but bonded couples are said to be able to communicate that way. The longer the couple is together, the stronger the bond is said to grow."

"Bonded couples? You mean married people?"

Jarden nodded. "When they marry, some bind themselves together, body and spirit. It involves the drinking of a special potion and the sharing of life force. It is said it can be dangerous, though not terribly so between elves."

"But how could this be the same thing? They aren't married, and Elora never drank anything."

Jarden shrugged. "It might not be the same thing. But when the elf cast the curse, he did bind her love to it. Perhaps the result was similar in some way. But that can be explored later. For now, I need to know about the princess's feelings toward Adrian. If she doesn't love him. If you don't think she ever will, then I need to tell the king of my suspicions. If she does love him—I don't know what I should do."

"I don't know." Deanna stared off into the distance. "Let me talk to her. I'll be careful what I say," she said as Jarden began to protest. "I'll just feel her out."

"Very well," he said. "Meet me here tomorrow at the same time to give your report."

"Yes, sir," Deanna said with a laugh, giving him a mock salute.

With a scowl, he turned and walked away. There was a man she could quite enjoy messing with, she thought as she headed off in the other direction.

Deanna removed her long, white gloves and cute, pink shoes and plopped back on the bed. Elora wrinkled her nose at her friend. Deanna was so carefree and exuberant in all she did. Elora tried to imagine what it would have been like if their roles were reversed, and Deanna were the princess instead.

"What do you think you would have done?" Elora asked her as she sat on the window seat. "If this had happened to you instead?"

"Hmm." Deanna hummed softly as she took her time to think over the question. "First off, I don't envy you." She said,

"What do you mean?" Elora's laugh was void of humor. "Everyone wants to be a princess."

"Not one who lives under the threat of a curse." Deanna wriggled her eyebrows at her.

"Who doesn't love a good curse?" Elora replied dryly. "It always ends in a prince or a knight coming to save the poor damsel in distress. At least, I hope it does." She played with the curtain tassel, winding it around her hand as she stared out the window.

"Or a soldier named Adrian?" suggested Deanna.

Elora turned to her and sighed. "I don't know. Could I be overthinking it? I just..." She glanced back at the window, the rolling hills and countryside a welcome respite from her tumultuous thoughts.

Deanna sat up in the bed and crossed her legs under her. "Let's examine the question, shall we?"

Elora smiled at her matter-of-fact tone.

"You think he's attractive?"

"Yes."

"You like being around him and talking to him."

"Yes."

"Whenever you see him, your heart speeds up, and a tingle runs through your body."

"Um. Well, no. Not really."

"Nothing?"

Elora shook her head.

Deanna rested her chin on her hands. "It sounds like you don't love him then."

"But I could grow to love him. Right? All the ingredients are there, aren't they?"

"Sure," replied Deanna doubtfully. Should she say something?

"Oh, who am I kidding?" Elora shoved herself off the seat and began pacing the room. "I don't love him. It's only been desperate hope that's made me think I might. The elf said I couldn't love, and he's right." *Stupid elf!* She sent the thought through their link with all the power she had, and she felt confident he heard her. Even though he didn't respond, a feeling of annoyance traveled back to her.

"But don't you think the possibility is there? You still have a week."

"There's something about him. It's almost like he's too charming. You know what I mean?" She stopped pacing and crossed her arms. "There's something almost not quite genuine about him." She waved her arms in the air. "Maybe I'm just reading too much into it. He's probably just trying too hard."

Deanna glanced away and remained silent. Elora narrowed her eyes at this unusual behavior. "What do you know?"

"What? What do you mean? I don't know anything."

"Yes, you do. Tell me."

Deanna bit her bottom lip. "Well, it's just that you're not the first person today who's said he seems a little off."

Elora's brows shot up in surprise. "Who else said that?"

"Jarden. He didn't want to say anything that might influence you if you were falling in love with him, but he's concerned. Don't tell him I told you."

"What does he suspect him of?"

"He said that he acted strangely during the failed ambush, and he thought he heard him talking to someone in his room earlier."

Elora walked over to the fireplace and watched the flames dance.

"What are you going to do?" asked Deanna.

"I'm meeting him after lunch. He said he wanted to talk to me. I'll ask him about it."

"No! You can't! If he is the spy Jarden thinks he might be, he could hurt you. He certainly won't let you go if he knows you don't trust him."

"I have to," said Elora, turning to face Deanna. "I have to know."

"Why would he even tell you the truth?"

"I don't know that he will, but if he's guilty, he'll probably give some excuse." She walked over and sat on the bed beside her friend. "That might give us some clue. But if he is innocent, he deserves a chance to defend himself. Everyone deserves that."

"Shall I go with you? I can hide somewhere nearby. Just in case?"

Elora huffed. "No, thank you. I'll be fine. I'm not some helpless damsel in distress even if I will soon need a handsome prince to come and rescue me."

Deanna gave her friend a sad smile and patted her hand.

"I have to go away for a little while."

Panic rose in Elora's chest. She had already decided that she didn't love him, but the thought of Adrian not being here, of there being no opportunity for love to grow, filled her with anxiety. He was her last chance.

"Where are you going?" she asked.

"I have a lead I want to follow up on about the curse."

He was still trying to help her. That thought eased the pressure around her heart a little.

"What kind of lead?"

He shook his head. "I don't want to say more until I'm sure. It might not be anything. I don't want to get your hopes up."

How odd, she thought. He shouldn't have told her he had a lead if he didn't want to get her hopes up. Why, then, would he not tell her what it was? His explanation didn't make sense. Or were Jarden's suspicions clouding her thinking?

"I plan to be back before your birthday. Will you save me a dance at the ball?" He ran his hand down her arm and locked his fingers through hers.

Elora tried to feel something through the contact. Was that a slight tingling in her stomach, or was it her imagination? Or was it fear at what she was about to do?

"Adrian," she said hesitantly, "tell me about the ambush attempt on the elves."

Adrian froze, his hand tightening around hers. "You've talked to Jarden, haven't you?" His voice was tight.

"No," she replied casually. "I'm just curious about what happened."

"That man has never liked me. Not from the beginning." He released her hand and turned away.

Elora touched his arm beseechingly. "Please tell me what happened."

He glanced at her over his shoulder and then turned back to face her. "I saw them," he said. "Do you remember I told you I had some magic that allowed me to follow Jarden undetected?"

Elora nodded.

"It's this amulet." he pulled a thick, round disk from inside his shirt. Runes and designs had been carved all over its surface. "It allows me to see a person's life force, even over great distances. Once I saw what Jarden's looked like, it was no problem following him from miles back."

"What did it show you about the elves?"

"The strength of their power is tied to their life forces. The greater the force, the stronger the power. As I said, I saw them. Not their faces, their power. They were all incredibly strong. I knew instantly that we wouldn't stand a chance. Even in an ambush, taking them by surprise, we wouldn't stand a chance."

"Did you tell Jarden?"

He laughed and turned away again, walking to a window, his eyes focused on the horizon. "What do you think he would say?"

"He would want to try anyway," she replied sadly.

He strode back to her, grabbing her hands in his, his eyes locked on hers. "He would, and they would have slaughtered us. I had to think of some way to stop it. Some way to save, if not all of our men, at least a few of them." His eyes pleaded with hers for understanding. "The elves would be angry, but I thought if I warned them,"

Elora gasped and tried to pull her hands free, but he held tight.

"If I warned them, maybe they would expend their anger quickly. Maybe they would let some of us live. I begged them to, you know."

"You betrayed your company?" She still couldn't believe she was hearing him correctly.

"Don't you see? It was the only way. And it worked. Many of the men died, but they would have anyway. This way, some of us made it out alive. And more than that, I earned the trust of the elves. Now, if your curse can't be broken, I can use that trust to find answers or at least to get close to them. I'll kill the mage if I have to. Perhaps, with his death, you'll be free."

Elora didn't respond. He finally released her hands, and she pulled away, turning her back on him.

"We would all have died if I hadn't done it," he said helplessly.

She shot around. "You don't know that."

"I saw their power, Elora. I know."

She walked over to a tapestry hanging on the wall. Its heavy, thick fabric had been woven with intricate detail. She trailed her hand over the soft image of a soldier running his spear through the heart of an ogre. The smooth, luxurious feel contrasted sharply with the violent scene.

He walked up behind her and placed his hands on her shoulders. "Can you forgive me," his voice trembled with its intensity.

Could she? "I don't know, Adrian. It is a great deal to consider." She looked back at him over her shoulder. "Will you give me time to think about it?"

"I'm leaving in a few hours." He dropped his hands and stepped back. "I'm hoping you will know your heart before I return." She heard him move toward the door. "I have long thought that I might be able to break your curse, Elora. For my part, I still think that."

It wasn't until after he had gone that she remembered she had also wanted to ask him about what Jarden had overheard in the barracks. But it didn't matter, she decided. He would give another probable excuse for that as well. What it came down to was simple: did she trust him, or did she not?

Elora stood and watched out the window. A few moments later, she saw Adrian emerge from the castle and walk toward the barracks.

He lied to you. The voice intruded on her thoughts like a battering ram. It was him.

You're finally talking to me again.

She felt a strong sense of smugness and derision seeping through the bond.

Did you miss me?

She let all her anger bubble to the surface and sent it back to him. *No. Why are you talking to me again?*

I thought you should know that your boyfriend is lying to you.

What do you mean? How do you know?

I can hear your thoughts, remember? Or are you so stupid that you haven't figured that out yet?

Elora seethed. *Then, hear this thought.* She shot him an image of an elf having his head ripped off by a dragon, blood and gore dripping everywhere.

Tsk, tsk. That's a little violent for a princess, isn't it? Besides, that's not what I look like. Humor accompanied his words, and the emotion caused her anger to grow.

I don't care what you look like. Leave me alone.

Don't you want to know what he lied about?

No.

Your emotions betray you. I can feel your curiosity.

She grunted in frustration and hit the windowsill. He was right. She wanted to know. Not that she would trust an elf's word over a human's. *Fine. What did he lie about?*

He never asked us to spare his men. On the contrary, we told him we planned to kill them, and he didn't protest.

Why should I believe you?

Her words didn't spark any concern on the other end of the bond.

Believe me or not, I don't care. It is your kingdom that could suffer.

Then, why are you telling me this? You don't expect me to believe that you care about my kingdom.

Not at all. I would gladly watch it burn. I just thought you might like to know.

Suddenly, his reasoning dawned on her. *You want to make me doubt him because you're afraid he'll be able to break your curse.*

You foolish human. No one can break my curse. I made sure of that when I cast it.

Maybe, but I think you have some doubts. After all, it didn't exactly work the way you planned, did it? This time, she was the one to send derision back to him.

A shot of anger sparked to life in the back of her head. *Believe what you will. It will all end in a week's time, and you'll trouble me no more.*

The voice vanished, and all emotions disappeared as if a door had been slammed shut.

Chapter 9

Thorn and Edrym sat on wooden benches by the corner of the field as they sharpened their swords.

"I hate this as much as you do. She's driving us both crazy," said Edrym.

Thorn groaned. He felt selfish, always dragging his friends into his problems. But there was no other way. He'd spent most of his time with Edrym and his father, Elion, working to discover how the curse would affect him now that his bond with the human was so strong. And sparring or training with his friends whenever he got the chance. That was the best distraction.

"You did this to yourself," Lyariel said. She walked to the target and yanked an arrow out of it. She enjoyed reminding him of the innocence of his victim. After all, she loved to say, guilt is a healthy emotion when you've done something wrong.

"Don't act like they didn't have a part in it. This happened because of them," Thorn said, rehashing the old argument. A screeching pierced the air every time Edrym brushed the whetstone on the sword's edge. The sound did nothing to drown out the low murmur of the human's thoughts that were now a constant buzz in the back of his mind. She really needed to learn how to shutter them.

"And you cursed their child when she was just a baby. She had nothing to do with it," she retorted.

"I lost Ithil. It's only fair they lose something precious to them," he grumbled.

"Rumors say the castle's holding balls every night, now, in a last desperate attempt to find her true love. They've even begun inviting the soldiers and middle-class citizens."

Thorn turned to face him. His gaze was glued to his sword.

"It ends in a few nights," he responded. "She won't find anyone before then." He had waited a long time to see the curse fulfilled and would be glad when he finally had peace.

The sun had almost set, and the night drew nearer. Birds flew back to their homes as they chirped away, but it wasn't quiet outside. Thorn could hear the noise of other elves in the guild.

"We still have no idea if it'll affect you too," Edrym said. Elion had not been able to determine the extent to which Thorn's error in the spell would pull him into the curse. It worried him a bit.

"We'll find out soon," Lyariel whispered, taking another shot. The arrow struck the center. "Elion is the wisest of the mages. If an answer is out there, he'll discover it."

"And what if an answer is not out there?"

"Bullseye," a soft, feminine voice broke the silence that followed Thorn's question. He glanced at the young elf girl as she stood beside Edrym. Her red hair was braided into two pigtails. Her black shirt was neatly tucked into her breeches, and her boots had been polished to a shine.

132

"She's been training a lot and gotten a good deal better with her bow," Edrym replied.

"But not as good as Thorn, I bet."

Edrym snorted at Lyariel's little sister's obvious infatuation.

"Is your human princess messing with you again?" Freyah asked as she tugged on her braids and sat down on the bench next to Thorn.

"All week." Thorn stood, reaching for his quiver. He pulled out an arrow and steadied it on the bow. His eyes narrowed on the target as he pulled the bow taut.

"Argh," he grunted. The arrow flew out of his grip and missed the target. It landed on the wooden fence surrounding the training field.

"Not quite better than Lyariel, eh?" Edrym slapped the little girl on the back. Thorn groaned.

"It's her again. She's shouting at me now."

"That seems a bit petty," said Edrym.

"As petty as reading boring texts to her night and day?" asked Lyariel. "Yes, I heard about that."

Edrym chuckled.

"I needed to review that material," said Thorn. A small smile played at the corners of his mouth. "It is valuable information that everyone should know. I was doing her a favor projecting it to her."

"Valuable information?" said Lyariel with a laugh. "The shelf life of ancient medical herbs?"

"You never know when that knowledge might come in handy. And, besides, I gave her breaks occasionally. I hear her all the time now."

"She's a human," protested Lyariel. "She doesn't know how to block her thoughts."

"What does she think about?" asked Freyah.

Thorn considered his answer, reflecting on the conversations he had paid attention to. "Now that the man Adrian is gone, she's been spending most of her time with various other men. She is exerting great effort in her attempt to like them. She's thinking only positive things about each one she's with, but her emotions give her away."

Lyariel shivered a little at the wicked grin that marred his features. "You really hate her, don't you?"

"I hate them all," he replied, "but the way she's been taunting me lately certainly hasn't endeared her to me."

"How about a sparring match," suggested Lyariel suddenly. "That should take your mind off it." She grabbed the spear Edrym laid beside the bench. Edrym stood, swinging his sword in well-practiced arcs.

"Loser buys dinner," she added. The men nodded in response and took their positions. Freyah sat down on the bench to watch.

Lyariel's green eyes shifted between Edrym and Thorn. She thrust the spear forward, testing their reflexes. Thorn's hand rested on his quiver. Edrym lunged at them with his sword raised. Thorn pulled out an arrow as Lyariel ran toward them with the two halves of the spear. He shot. She swatted the arrow away before it met her and rammed the spear into Edrym's sword. Thorn's fingers twitched as he reached for another arrow.

Suddenly, a song burst out in the back of his mind. He recognized the voice. Elora was listening to her friend, Deanna, sing. Very loudly.

In realms where darkness dares to tread,

I'll share my scorn for beings bred,
The elves, so smug in their ancient might,
I'll cast their image in a different light.

With pointed ears and airs so grand,
They dwell in forests, a snooty band,
Their arrogance, like a silver thread,
Weaves through their tales of greatness spread.

They prance and preen in the moonlight's glow,
With voices like breezes that softly blow,
But underneath their graceful façade,
Lies a shallow race, forever flawed.

He tried to ignore the song as he dodged a thrust of Lyariel's spear, shifting just in time.

"You're getting slower," she said as she jabbed both halves of the spear toward Edrym and Thorn. Edrym stopped the spear with his sword and pushed into her.

"La sanden stige," Thorn said. A great cloud of dust formed and obscured her vision as he shoved her spear out of the way with his bow. Lyariel flipped backward.

"Sterk vind blåse," she sang. Edrym and Thorn flew to the ground. Thorn felt a sting in his head as he coughed, waving off the dust. Lyariel was a skilled fighter, even without her magic. With it, she was ruthless. But he could beat her. If only he could concentrate.

They're ageless, yes, but what's the cost?
A life devoid of what they've lost,
For mortal trials, they'll never know,
No scars of time to help them grow.

135

In their ivory towers, they dwell aloof,
Mocking us with each ageless proof,
But in their perfection, they're so naïve,
Unaware of the world they deceive.

So, let me jest at their hollow grace,
And laugh at the smiles on their elven face,
For in their elegance, so tightly wound,
I find a race with no substance found.

Thorn growled and shook his head, trying to rid his mind of the annoying melody.

He's getting angry. He heard a different voice in the back of his mind. A voice that had become all too familiar lately. *Keep going.*

I hate their kind, so full of guile,
Their promises, a treacherous smile,
They lure with gifts and silver tongue,
But beneath the charm, their poison wrung.

Thorn tried to pull himself off the ground but stopped as he felt the pain again. Worse. Lyariel pointed the spear's head at his throat, pinning him to the ground. While Edrym had his sword raised under her jaw.

"I'm going to kill her," Thorn roared. "I don't care that the curse will go into effect in a few days. I can't wait. I'm going to kill her now." He pulled his dagger from its sheath and began to disappear.

"Wait a minute," Edrym and Lyariel both grabbed his arms. He could transport himself to the human castle, but with his mind in its current state, he didn't have the concentration and focus to take all three of them.

"Deep breaths," said Lyariel. "Calm down. You're giving her the reaction she wants. Don't let her have the satisfaction of riling you."

"I thought you were on her side," he said with a glare.

"I think what you did was unfair to the poor girl, but you're my friend, not her. I'll stand by you when you need it."

"Here," said Edrym, shoving an ax at him. "We need some firewood for dinner."

Thorn glared at his friend. "No, we don't."

Edrym crossed his arms. "Well, pretend we do. You must work out your frustration somehow, and we can never have too much firewood."

Edrym was right about him needing to work out his frustration, but when he went to bed a couple of hours later, he was pretty sure his friend was wrong about not being able to have too much firewood. The pile he left could last the whole elven community weeks.

Goblin mage Vrek opened the door to the messenger's knock.

"Yes, what did he say?"

"The king has agreed to an audience. He and the princess await you in the king's office, eager to see what new remedies you have to try," the messenger said.

Vrek glanced at his guards, Bral and Briq, as he left. They nodded and moved to a door at the back of the room.

As the pair stepped through the door, it closed softly behind them, leaving them in the dimly lit chamber that was their makeshift headquarters beneath the castle. The space was abuzz with activity, the air thick with the haze of goblin magic. Some goblins sat around rough-hewn tables, hungrily devouring stolen morsels from the human kitchens. Others sharpened their swords and knives, the glint of steel reflecting in their eyes. A few meticulously crafted bows and arrows while others engaged in hushed conversations, strategizing their impending mission.

Two figures entered the room through another entrance, carrying trays of food. At first glance, they appeared to be ordinary human servants, their attire blending seamlessly with the castle staff. However, as soon as the door closed behind them, they dropped their glamor spells, revealing their true goblin forms. Their green-tinted skin and sharp features left no doubt as to their species.

The room was dimly lit, with the flickering light of candles and torches casting eerie shadows on the walls, giving it an air of secrecy and conspiracy. It was here, in the underground heart of the castle, that the goblins had gathered. Using their glamor magic, they had snuck into the castle, two by two, disguised as various people Vrak, Bral, and Briq had met through their explorations. Here, they concealed themselves, waiting for their moment to strike.

Bral and Briq wasted no time. They made their way to a large wooden table at the center of the room, where a detailed map of the castle was laid out. Candlelight danced upon the parchment. They began discussing the castle's layout with hushed voices, focusing on the paths leading to the princess's chamber.

"We need to find a route that will allow a few people to see us, preferably servants," Bral muttered, his eyes fixed on the map's labyrinthine corridors. "But we must avoid running into too many guards."

Briq nodded in agreement, his eyes scanning the layout of the castle. "A few witnesses among the servants would be ideal. We need rumors to spread quickly."

Together, they analyzed the various passageways and secret passages they had discovered during their weeks of clandestine activity within the castle. The tension in the room was palpable as they weighed their options, knowing that their plan needed to be executed flawlessly.

"The kitchen staff usually retire early," Bral mused, tracing a path with his finger. "We can let the rest of the soldiers in through there, disguised as human servants finishing up their duties for the night."

Briq considered this, then pointed to a narrow corridor leading toward the princess's chambers. "And from there, one group can slip into this corridor. A few guards are always there, and servants regularly pass by. The guards will need to be killed, but make sure the men don't harm the servants, at least, not much. We want them to live to tell of the *elves'* invasion." His laugh shook the room.

"The humans won't hesitate to join us in our war against the pointy-eared pests after they kill their precious princess," said Bral with a sneer.

Their plan took shape on the map. The princess would fall under the curse before long, and as soon as things died down, they would be ready to act.

Elora lost count of the men she'd walked with, talked with, and danced with the last few days. They were all very different in personality and appearance, but none of them made a lasting impression. She wished desperately that Adrian would return soon. He was the only one she might have a chance with. She just had one more day. Tomorrow was it.

Her last chance.

Her last hope.

Without love, she would sleep forever. She had just come from her father's office, where she had insisted on meeting with him and his advisors. She knew her father. He would expend all his time and energy on finding a cure, but they had been searching all her life. If a cure were to be found, it would have been by now. She had to convince him to move on. The kingdom was more important than one person, even a princess.

She had told them to bring the twins to the castle. He must work with them both, the eldest to prepare him for his reign and the youngest to prepare him for his role as chief advisor and to convince him to be content with it. He had reluctantly agreed. Perhaps things would work out.

She went to bed that night with a heavy heart. She wanted to accept her fate and be strong, and she did, mostly, but a small part of her, a selfish part, wanted to live, even if it was a life without love. She reached out to the elf. Since nothing else had worked, she would attempt to appeal to his sympathy.

Please, she whispered in her mind, using all her strength to send the words across the distance to him. *Please stop this.* She wrapped the plea in all her sorrow, pain, and distress. She soaked it in desperation and despair, tears coursing down her cheeks. *I'm sorry for what my kingdom did. I'm so, so sorry for the pain you have suffered. But please don't do this. Please help me. Please. Please.* She finally fell asleep, her pillow soaked with tears and the words echoing through their bond.

Miles away, over the mountains and through the forest, Thorn froze, his hand hovering over the page he had been about to turn. He clenched his jaw and glared at the bookshelf across from him. Such grief, such pain. Pity sprang up in his heart, but he immediately crushed it. He hardened his resolve. He couldn't think in the onslaught of such overwhelming emotion, so he sat there, immobile, and waited for it to pass.

Tomorrow, she turned eighteen.

Tomorrow, the curse would take hold.

Tomorrow, her life would end.

The gray clouds obscuring the sun echoed the gloom that had settled over the entire kingdom. Everyone knew the significance of this day. And everyone mourned as if the worst had already come to pass.

Elora had insisted that she spend this last day with her family and friends. She couldn't talk her mother out of a final ball, but the day was hers. She began that morning with a long, solitary ride, and during that ride, she thought.

Not of her quickly approaching fate but of her kingdom. She thought of the problems they faced and suggestions she could give her father for improvement. She thought of her cousins and how the youngest might be convinced to accept his brother on the throne. She thought of her mother and her friends and how she could ease their grief at her loss.

When she returned to the castle, she met with her father, and they discussed her ideas. Some had potential, others didn't, but he was proud of her, and he told her so.

"You would have made a wonderful queen." Tears softly streamed down his face. She flung herself into his arms.

"I'll miss you so much, Daddy."

"I'll miss you, too, my little flower."

They stayed that way until the queen, who had been looking for her, walked in and joined them. The three spent a precious time together. Elora steered their conversation away from the impending sorrow to happier days they'd had in the past.

They relived memories of her childhood. She'd confessed to mischievous acts she and Deanna had gotten away with. They shared their joys and hopes and even the small fears that every parent has when their child is growing up. The only thing the three didn't talk about was the curse.

Finally, it was time for lunch, and they walked into the dining hall hand in hand. As they had all morning, various servants and guards lined the hallways everywhere she walked. Tears streamed down many faces, and sniffles softly sounded in the background. They all loved her. This was their way of honoring her last day and saying goodbye.

After lunch, Elora retired to her chamber with Roe and Deanna. That night's ball was to be the grandest of all, and she must be dazzling. Deanna had a hoard of servants coming and going with no aim but to pamper her as she'd never been pampered before.

A luxurious bubble bath with musicians playing quietly in the next room.

A soothing massage.

A manicure and pedicure. The works.

Elora enjoyed it all, but her favorite was when the other servants left, and she could be alone with her friends. They, too, talked of olden days: when they'd met, the fun times they'd had together. It was a happy sorrow that enveloped them, and the tears they cried went ignored as they each tried to be strong for the others.

Roe was going to the ball that night as well. Elora had insisted on it, so they all got ready together. The trio left Elora's chambers arm in arm and headed to the ballroom.

Adrian was back.

He was the first person she saw when she walked through the huge double doors. And he hurried over to her, arms extended. She felt the weight of everyone's gaze as he approached. A silence had fallen over the room as if all the attendees collectively held their breaths. Roe and Deanna gave the princess a sad glance and released her, backing away.

A light shone in his eyes. His whole face, in fact, seemed to glow with excitement. Could it be? Could he really love her? Maybe...

"My dear Elora, I missed you so."

"Hello, Adrian."

He deflated somewhat when her enthusiasm didn't match his own, but he rallied quickly.

"Come, let's dance."

She took his hand, and they danced. She gave herself up to the motions, to the music. She felt it like she'd never felt it before. She let it invade her very being.

No thoughts.

No worries.

No sorrow.

She became one with the music. And danced.

She lost track of time. She had no idea how long they'd been on the dance floor. She was only awoken from her trance by the ache slowly, insistently making itself known in her feet. She needed to stop. To rest.

Adrian hadn't said a word to her as they moved to the music. He understood that she needed this. But he spoke up then.

"Shall we take a break in the garden? We can rest by the fountain."

Elora nodded, and they made their way outside. As they walked through the garden toward the fountain, all the couples outside quietly made their way in. Everyone wanted to give her the best chance they could.

Elora started to ask him about where he had gone, but she hesitated. She didn't think he would tell her. That thought grated on her nerves a bit, and she didn't want to ruin this peaceful night. Besides, he would say if he had discovered anything she needed to know.

"Tell me about your home," she said instead. It was a night for nostalgia, for looking back, not forward.

They sat there and talked for hours, the water splashing gently in the fountain and the stars twinkling overhead. Elora enjoyed the time she spent with him. She nurtured the tiny seed growing inside her. Maybe it would be enough.

Eventually, the music in the ballroom died down. It was late. She wanted to see her parents before she retired for the night. No one knew precisely when the curse would take effect. She might not even wake up the next morning.

"I should go."

Adrian brushed a strand of her hair behind her ear and chuckled. "Make sure you get your maid to fix your hair before you go to bed. It's all frizzy. You look a fright. You must look perfect when I kiss you awake, or it'll ruin the mood."

She remembered the conversation that she'd had with Roe over two months ago. If a man truly loved her, he would love her, frizzy hair and all. It was a flimsy reason to give up on love. But the thought of it opened her eyes to her true feelings. And just like that, all hope died. Elora gave him a weak smile, said 'goodnight,' and walked back into the ballroom alone.

The queen and king escorted her to her chambers, followed by Deanna and Roe and the entire court and guard and all the servants. She turned to face them when she reached her door. Adrian had made his way to the front, but she didn't single him out.

"I love you all so much," she said, smiling sadly to the group, tears tracing lines down her face, her chest heaving with her suppressed sobs. "I have one request of you all. I wish the best for you, and for that to be achieved, you must forget about me and move on with your lives. I will not be the cause of trouble coming to our kingdom through neglect. Promise me that you will move on."

Protests could be heard throughout the crowd, muffled by handkerchiefs and sobs.

"Promise me!" she insisted. "Please."

Soft whispers of "I promise" filled the corridor. She was satisfied.

With a brave smile, she wished them goodnight, opened the doors, and vanished into her room. The king, queen, Deanna, and Roe were the only ones to follow her. An entire platoon of guards took up posts outside her door and all down the hall as the crowd melted away.

"You've contacted the twins?" she asked her father as Roe took down her hair.

"Yes. They will arrive within the week." He sat beside her mother on the couch in her bedroom, his arm around the weeping woman, holding her close to his side.

"What about the merchants?"

"I have a meeting with the guild leaders next week. I'll present your ideas to them then."

There was no reason for this conversation, Elora knew. Her father had ruled the kingdom well enough without her help, but she was glad he humored her. To be honest, she didn't know what else to talk about. What do you say to your loved ones when you are

146

about to leave them forever? What can be said that will make any difference?

She moved behind the screen to change into her nightgown when a thought crossed her mind. In case she didn't wake up, perhaps it would be better if she changed into a dress. She didn't want to spend eternity on display in a nightgown, especially if people would be coming in to kiss her.

She had no doubt that her mother would have people come in and kiss her, as horrid as that thought was. She let Roe slip the nightgown over her head without saying anything. They could change her clothes later if they needed to. Roe would probably enjoy making her look beautiful while she slept. She would consider it a final act of service to her friend.

Elora yawned as she came back around the screen. Her mother saw her and jumped to her feet.

"Are you alright?" she asked frantically.

"I'm just a little sleepy. It is late." Elora's eyes grew heavy. It was late, but this exhaustion felt different than it should. It felt—more—somehow. "I should go to bed."

Queen Callista burst into a fresh torrent of tears. She threw herself into Elora's arms, weeping profusely. The king pulled her away and gave his daughter a hug and a kiss on the forehead. "Goodnight," he said, pulling his reluctant wife to the door.

Roe and Deanna hugged her as well before joining their monarchs.

"I'll see you in the morning," Elora said, giving them a last smile.

"See you in the morning," the king replied. Then he ushered them out the door, and she was alone.

Are you there? Elora sent the thought to the elf, but he didn't respond.

She walked over to her bed and stopped in surprise, staring at the item lying on her pillow. It was a single red rose. It hadn't been there before. She knew it hadn't. Someone would have seen it.

Her hand reached toward it as if it had a life of its own. At first, Elora struggled against it, but such a great weariness overcame her that she could resist no longer. She stretched out a finger and touched the soft petals. Then, her hand moved down and closed around the stem. A sharp thorn pierced the skin of one of her fingers. She sank to the floor, and her whole world went dark.

Chapter 10

Thorn spent the day in a melancholy mood. He should be happy. He was happy. This was the last day before the curse took effect. He would be free soon. But he couldn't enjoy his happiness. The princess was too sad.

It was her sadness seeping into his mind that he felt, not any empathetic response, he told himself. He rejoiced in her pain. If only he could feel the joy.

That night, he went to Elion and Edrym's house as planned. If the bond caused him to experience any effects of the curse, he needed to be there where they could help him. They spent a nice, relaxing evening together, eating and playing cards. It was very calm. The mood from his mind seemed to seep into their atmosphere. It was not the celebratory evening he had expected, but he could have fun the next day after all danger had passed.

Sometime in the middle of the night, Thorn began to feel strange. He looked at the clock. Midnight.

"Elion," he called, breathing heavily.

"What's wrong?" Edrym asked.

"It's almost time," Elion replied, laying his book on the table. "We need to get him to his room."

Elion and Edrym draped Thorn's heavy arms over their shoulders and walked him down the hall into the spare bedroom. The aroma of lavender greeted his nose, causing his already fuzzy brain to slip even farther away from his surroundings. He shook his head violently, causing some of the fogginess to recede.

"I can walk," he said, shrugging off their help. "It will help me stay awake." But his eyes felt heavy, and a great yawn stretched his face.

"You better stay awake, Thorn," Edrym said.

"I'm trying," he replied, shaking his head again. He pounded against his temples with his fists, but nothing helped this time.

"How do you feel?" Elion asked, touching his arm.

"It's close," he responded. He flickered his eyes as he fought to keep them open. His vision grew hazy.

"Don't worry, Buddy," said Edrym, slapping him on the back. "If you fall asleep, Freyah can kiss you and wake you up."

"Ha, ha." Thorn laughed. "I think I'd rather have Lyariel do it."

"Hmm," replied Edrym. "I don't think I'd like that."

Thorn harrumphed weakly. "I didn't think you would."

"I might just let you sleep if that's the alternative."

"You better not let me sleep. I expect the two of you to find some way to wake me up."

"We will. We will," reassured Elion.

His words faded in Thorn's ears, turning into whispers he couldn't make out. He felt an arm shake him, but he couldn't resist the heavy pressure on his eyelids. All images faded as he finally gave in to the curse. His last thought was of strong arms catching him and pushing him onto the bed.

Everything was dark at first, and then he thought he saw a shape, as of lighter shadows moving. Then, something suddenly brought him back. He jerked, and his eyes flew open. A stinging warmth spread across his cheek, and his palm instinctively rested on it.

"What was that for?" Thorn yelled at Edrym.

"You fell asleep. I couldn't think of any other way," he shrugged.

"Ouch," Thorn groaned.

"You're welcome," Edrym smirked.

"We have an answer now," Elion said, sitting on the rumpled bed.

Thorn rubbed his hands over his face. "Do you think it will last? What if I fall asleep again?"

"I have no problem hitting you as many times as I have to to keep you awake," Edrym joked.

"There won't be a need for that," Elion said with a thoughtful gaze.

"You should try to stay awake, though, till we are sure you can sleep without the curse affecting you long-term," he added. "How do you feel? Do you think you can? Are you still tired?"

Thorn pinched the bridge of his nose as he tried to remember what he'd seen when he slept.

"I saw something," He blurted. "But I can't remember what it was. It looked almost like a strange dream. But not," he added.

"It's probably nothing," Edrym responded.

"You slapped me out of it," he retorted.

"Again, you're welcome."

"And the bond?" Elion asked.

"I can't hear or feel anything. She must have fallen asleep," Thorn answered.

A moment of silence passed as he stared at the pillow. It was finally over. He was free of the bond. And he had avenged Ithil's death. But something felt wrong…

They were lined up all along the hall and down the stairs. People who loved her. It might not be the romantic love that the curse seemed to call for, but it was love nonetheless, and they would try. Adrian stood at the head of the line. Any true hope lay with him.

The queen sat by her bedside where she had been since they found the princess on the floor that morning. The king stood behind her, his hands resting comfortingly on her shoulders. The queen had immediately kissed her daughter's forehead the moment she saw her. Nothing had happened. Nor did it when the king, Deanna, and Roe followed suit.

Roe and Deanna helped the queen change her into the most beautiful gown she owned. They positioned her on the bed with her hair fanned out around her head and the fateful rose they had found lying on the floor beside her, clutched in her hands.

The queen had wanted to crush the hateful thing, but there was a sort of sadness in its beauty, as if it had performed the terrible deed against its will. In a way, it reminded her of the princess, so she decided to let it have its place with her.

Adrian waited impatiently with so many others for the door to open. If he couldn't awaken Elora, there was no use for anyone else to try. But the king and queen had decided to allow their subjects, lined up outside, to give the princess their own kisses of goodbye. As a final salute before they all honored their promise and went on with their lives.

King Leopold motioned for the honor guard to let Adrian enter. He walked over to the bed and shifted uncomfortably under the stares of her family and friends. He wished they would leave him to do this in peace. It seemed like a sacred moment that others shouldn't share. But he knew they wouldn't leave. He focused on her face and attempted to ignore their presence behind him. She looked more beautiful than he had ever seen her. Strong emotions swirled in his chest as he slowly bent down over her.

He knew they expected him to kiss her on the forehead or the cheek, but he wouldn't pass up this opportunity. This was love, true love. It deserved a proper kiss. He gently placed his lips against her own, feeling a thrill rush through him at the pressure. He so desperately wanted to extend the moment, but it wouldn't be proper. He rose and watched her, expecting her eyes to flutter open at any moment. But they didn't. Only her shallow breath caused any movement in her body.

Crushing disappointment overwhelmed him. What had happened? He had been so sure. He hung his head in shame. What must the king and queen think? And all those people outside. They would know. She hadn't loved him.

In utter defeat, he made his way down the corridor, carrying despair in his wake as each person he passed realized he had failed.

Adrian walked out of the castle and to the barracks. He loaded the few possessions he had brought into his saddlebag, went to the stables, saddled his horse, and rode out of the city, never to return.

Thorn took a deep breath as he approached the castle at the heart of Allanar. Its tall spires reached toward the sky, competing with the ancient redwoods that grew around it. A clear stream ran nearby, the bubble of its water echoed by the elegant fountain in the lush garden beside it.

Intricate carvings marked the entrance, protection spells that no man could pass unwanted. Two elf guards stood at the entrance with their hands resting lightly on their swords.

Thorn knew why he had been summoned. He had thought his troubles ended when his curse was finally fulfilled. Unfortunately, they had only begun.

He had not slept for four days. And while elves could quite easily go for long periods without sleep, he felt the lack keenly. Deep down, he feared sleep. Though he would never admit it. He feared he would not be able to wake up.

His eyes felt heavy as he bowed before the king.

"Your Majesty," he said respectfully.

"Rise, Thornindell Greenbow," the elven king responded, waving his hand airily. He leaned in his seat and placed his arm on the armrest. The sunlight streaming in from the many windows sent sparkles off his gold and diamond crown. His long black hair hung over deep purple robes that matched his eyes, and his strong jawline added to his imposing presence.

"Your Majesty." One of the elders sitting along the side of the room stood to his feet. "Is this not the mage that cursed the human princess?" His gray eyes glared at Thorn.

"Yes, it is. And that is why I have called you here today," the king replied. He shifted in his chair as he stared at the elf waiting in the middle of the room.

"How may I be of assistance, Your Majesty?"

"The human princess has fallen into a deep sleep, as I am sure you are aware?"

"Yes, Your Majesty," he responded.

"Their king, Leopold, is troubled about his daughter's state and had invited me to the castle," he said.

Thorn blinked his eyes groggily. He mustn't fall asleep here, of all places.

"What you can do to be of assistance," he continued, "is find some way to break the curse."

"But, Your Majesty," Thorn said helplessly, "as you know, once a curse is enacted, it cannot be broken except by fulfilling its requirements."

"Nevertheless, you must find a way."

"If you cannot, we will have another war on our hands," another elder said.

"It is not just a war with the goblins we must worry about, but now, because of your reckless actions, we may have a war with the humans, too. We wouldn't have a chance against both kingdoms," added the first elder.

"Break the curse and awaken the princess. Save the elven race, and you will be rewarded for it. Greatly," the king added.

Thorn swallowed hard. He didn't know how to break the curse. Only true love's kiss could save her, and it was already too late for that. His mind whirled, trying to think of some solution. Any solution.

"Thorn," the king called after a few moments of silence.

"I cannot break the curse, your Majesty," he said.

"Are you objecting to the king's order?" another elder asked, outrage seeping from his tone.

"Never, Your Majesty." A great silence filled the room. Thorn could hear his heartbeat quicken as he stood before the king, waiting for his response.

"Filvendor!" the king said.

"Your Majesty," the guard on his left answered, jerking to attention.

"Summon all the mages in the kingdom for a council and all the officers for a war meeting. For war will be upon us if the council cannot find a solution," the king ordered.

What have I done...

"Edrym," Thorn called as he banged on the door to his friend's house.

"Edrym," he called out again. Darkness had fallen, but he knew Edrym and his family would not be asleep yet.

He could not stay awake anymore. His eyes drooped, and his body begged for relief.

Five days without sleep had almost driven him crazy. He had been taking a potion to help him stay awake, but its effects had gradually diminished until it did nothing for him anymore.

"Thorn?" Edrym asked as he peeped through the window. "What's wrong?"

"I need your help." Thorn yawned.

Edrym unlocked the door to let him in.

"I can't do it anymore. I have to sleep."

Elion walked out of a side room with his spectacles on and a book in his hand. Thorn smiled at the familiar sight. He felt a bit delirious.

"Thorn, is all well?" Elion asked. He looked intently at Thorn's face and placed a hand against his forehead.

"He can't stay awake anymore," Edrym said as he disappeared into the pantry.

Thorn perched on the edge of a chair and rubbed his eyes with the back of his hand.

"Then you should have your night's rest here," Elion offered.

"But the curse." Thorn retorted. Edrym returned with an apple in his hand and offered it to him. Thorn wasn't hungry, but he took it anyway. Perhaps the act of eating would help him stay awake a little longer.

"That's why we have Freyah to save you," Edrym chuckled. Elion ignored his son.

"I'll watch you and help if anything happens," Elion said. Thorn's sleepy eyes were slowly shutting. He started to take a bite of the apple but felt it fall from his hands. He batted his eyelids, trying to keep himself awake for a few more seconds. But he had no strength left.

"Thorn," Edrym said as he shook his arm.

"Take him to the guest room," said Elion.

157

Edrym gripped his arm and pulled him up. His body weighed a ton. This was not normal exhaustion.

"The king wants me to break the curse, but I don't know how," Thorn blurted out as he walked down the hallway.

"We'll talk about it on the morrow," Edrym responded as he opened the door to the bedroom. Thorn fell on the bed and sighed heavily, his eyes falling closed. He thought he felt a sting on his cheek just before everything went dark. Then he felt nothing.

Darkness filled the night. Not the darkness that was common with the absence of day but an all-encompassing, pervading darkness that seemed to seep into his very bones. No stars twinkled in the sky. No light gleamed from the silent houses nearby. It was as if all illumination had been forever banished from the earth.

And yet, he could see.

Gray shadows in the shape of trees waved in a non-existent wind. Buildings, a slightly darker gray, surrounded him. The whole earth seemed awash in shades of gray.

"Hello." His words echoed through the empty town. Mocking his aloneness. He shivered as a chill raced down his spine. He could hear his heavy breaths as his chest heaved.

"Am I dreaming?" he murmured into the night.

Thorn squeezed his eyes closed. Then quickly opened them, hoping he would be awake and among familiar surroundings once again. He glanced around at the stone walls. *He was in a castle. A human castle by the look of it. He gasped. The princess's castle, he would bet his best sword.*

The damp and cold seeped through his clothes as if he were naked. A movement out of the corner of his eye caught his attention. His elven senses tingled. He wasn't alone. This castle had figures that hid in the dark—shadows shifting as he walked down the hall. He rested his hand on his dagger, thankful he hadn't taken it off when he fell asleep.

When he fell asleep. That's right. He must be dreaming. He was sleeping in Elion's guest room. Was this an effect of the curse or just the strangest dream he had ever experienced?

A voice sounded down the corridor and made him pause. Someone was there. Someone real. The realization was both soothing and alarming. He didn't know what or who to expect.

He continued cautiously in the same direction and heard the voice again. Clearer now. They were crying. Thorn could not mistake the gasps and sniffs. Soft sobs ending in small quivers, indicative of deep sorrow, reached out to him as he hurried forward.

Surely, this couldn't be who he knew it had to be.

He walked further into the castle, following the sound until he saw her. There she was, huddled on the floor, in a corner under a window. Her white dress pooled on the ground around her.

She didn't notice his presence. Her head rested buried in her hands. Thorn hadn't seen the princess since she was an infant, but he recognized her. Her sorrow was palpable and familiar. He had felt it too many times before not to recognize it now.

He melted back into the shadows and stared transfixed at the girl. Was this to be his fate, then? Was he cursed as well? Must he forever visit her when he slept? To watch her in her misery. Is this his punishment for bringing such a fate upon an innocent girl? For as much as he argued otherwise with Lyariel, he knew the girl was innocent.

But maybe he was wrong. Maybe this wasn't the cursed princess. Maybe he had gotten caught in another spell. There were many mages who wouldn't mind seeing him suffer for the threat of war he had brought to his people. Maybe one of them did this. He had to know.

He cleared his throat and stepped into the lighter gray. The girl gasped. She raised her head sharply and met his gaze. She was human. Thorn wasn't surprised to discover that, but still, maybe.

An unusual emotion hit him so strongly that it took his breath away. It felt like someone had punched him in the stomach.

The girl's red-rimmed eyes were piercing as she stared unflinchingly at him.

From nowhere, he felt a wave of pain, loneliness, bitterness, and anger that left his insides in a mess. Were these emotions coming from her? Still, maybe...

They stared at each other, not blinking for what seemed like an eternity.

"Who are you?" he finally asked. He had to know for sure.

"Who are you?" she croaked, staring defiantly at him. She lifted her head higher, jutting out her chin and raising her nose in the air.

She was brave, he thought.

"What is this place?" he changed the question since she refused to answer the first.

"I wish I knew," came the reply.

That grabbed his attention. "You don't know where we are?"

She shrugged at that, wiping her eyes with the back of her hands. "Do you?"

"How did you get here?" Thorn asked. He had to find out. He had to know.

"I fell asleep," she said.

There were no more maybes. He could no longer deny it.

She must have seen the recognition in his eyes because she snapped. "Do you know me?"

Thorn felt his heart stop as he stared at her in shock. He hadn't expected her to be so beautiful. Even in the shaded gray that dulled everything there, she was beautiful. But that didn't matter. She was a human, the daughter of the enemy.

The stupid bond he'd formed in his foolishness had linked them together in the curse as well. A frightening thought crossed his mind. If the bond had brought him to her here, then he might sleep forever, too. He had no true love to kiss him awake. Would he be stuck here with her for eternity?

"Do you know me?" She repeated warily. "Who are you?"

Not bothering to answer her questions, he turned and walked away. He had to wake up. He could not be stuck here. He would never allow it. Not with her. The castle door came into sight as he headed toward it. He would find some way out of this mess. If nothing else, he could walk back to Allanar in this dream world. If he

161

couldn't wake, then he could at least spend the remainder of his life among his own people.

When he reached the enormous doors at the entrance to the castle, he pulled them open and stepped through. But he wasn't outside. He looked around, confused.

The dull tapestries on the stone walls looked familiar, as did the corridor. A sound reached his ears. It was the girl. She wasn't crying now, but an occasional sniffle interrupted her unsteady breathing. He didn't show himself to her. Instead, he turned and tried again.

And again.

And again.

But the results were the same. He would not be leaving the castle.

He gave up on his futile attempts to escape and showed himself to the princess. He needed information if he were to have any chance of escape.

The way she regarded him was different now, and he knew she'd figured out who he was somehow. The hatred that filled her eyes was mutual.

"You're the elf mage, aren't you?" she said quietly. "The one that cursed me."

Thorn didn't respond.

"You're the one, aren't you?" Her quiet voice was now soaked in disgust, and that bothered him. Even more than anger or hatred.

He still refused to give her a response. He just watched her. It was odd. At times, he could feel her emotions, but he couldn't hear her thoughts.

"Answer me," She hissed. Some of her anger seeped into him. This time around, he welcomed it. It was the only point of familiarity in this strange world. But he didn't like her authoritarian tone.

He turned and walked away again. He would get nothing from her in this mood. He would have to find the answers for himself. This time, he headed in the opposite direction. He found some stairs and climbed them to the top of a tower.

Standing at a window, he could see for miles. The same dull gray colored this landscape. He looked down at the great distance to the ground. The rough stone wall would be difficult to climb but not impossible.

He stepped up on the windowsill and grabbed the edge. He wished he had found a window on a lower floor, but this was the only one he had run across so far, and he didn't dare miss this opportunity.

He lowered his leg and found a foothold. Easing his body off the ledge, he began to descend. He knew the princess had followed him. He had sensed her presence as he wandered the halls, so it was no surprise when he glanced up and saw her head peek out the window. He continued his descent undisturbed.

Finally, his hands cut and blistered, his feet sore, he reached the ground. But the second he set his foot onto the welcome dirt, it changed to stone, as did the trees around him. He was back in the tower room. The princess leaned against a wall, her arms crossed and a smirk gracing her beautiful face.

Thorn growled and stomped out of the room. Within a few hours, he had mapped out the castle and its boundaries. The princess had followed him the entire time. She offered no help, but neither did she get in his way. In fact, she said nothing at all. Her emotions were quiet as well.

The space they had to share was small but not too small. If they were stuck here forever, they could work it out. He would take the west wing, and she could have the east. He turned to offer that compromise when his surroundings began to fade. He looked at the princess. She held a hand out to him.

"No," she cried as she faded away.

Elion stood before him with a candle held up to his face. Thorn wiped the beads of sweat that had formed on his brow.

"What happened?" Elion asked.

"I saw her. I saw the princess."

Chapter 11

Freyah winked at Thorn as she sat beside Edrym. All the elven mages in Allanar had to be present in the council meeting hall. As one of the mage elders, Elion sat at the front of the room. Whispers filled the air as everyone waited for the meeting to begin.

Guilt surged through Thorn as he sat on the edge of one of the wooden benches that lined the room. Not guilt for cursing the princess, exactly, but guilt for bringing this danger to his people. Everyone was aware of the trouble at hand. Worse, everyone knew it was because of him.

The last of the mages finally arrived. They could begin.

"Welcome," said Elion, his deep voice carrying the weight of his authority. "The King has summoned us all..."

"We know why we're here," a mage spoke up from the back of the room.

"All thanks to Thorn trying to get his revenge," another voice said from the crowd. Thorn turned to meet an intense gaze from Vasper. His hatred toward him wasn't a mystery. Elion had chosen to train Thorn instead of the other elf, and Vasper had resented him ever since.

"This is no time to dwell on the past. What was done was done. Now, we must find our path forward. The king demands we discover a way to break the curse," Elion replied. He glanced at Thorn and then back to the people.

Thorn stood from his bench and faced the elders. "I have something to say."

"Speak," Elion said.

Thorn took a deep breath. "I had a dream about the princess," he announced. The mages turned to look at each other, confused.

"As many of you know, I created a bond between the princess and myself when I placed the curse on her. The bond has grown stronger. The other night, I slept for the first time since the curse took effect, and I dreamed of her."

"And what did you see?" Elion asked for the benefit of the others.

"I saw her in a castle. A human castle. I believe it to be her own. But it was dark there in the dream world. There was no color. Everything was in varying shades of gray."

He went on to explain all he had seen and discovered. "I believe it was more than a simple one-sided dream. I believe the bond has taken me to her to where her mind dwells while she is under the curse."

Gasps filled the room at this news. Elion held up his hand for silence.

"At least we know she is alive," he said.

"But the dream does not tell us how to save her," one mage said. She stood up to speak. Her black hair stopped at her chin, but her eyes reminded Thorn of Elora's.

"What exactly were the words you spoke?" she asked.

"I morgen attende bursdag jeg forbanner deg å falle ned i et dyp Når en rosetorn," Thorn said, trying to remember the rest. He had mixed up the spell. "Skal prikke slikkepott og jeg skaper et bånd...med deg å bli ødelagt av ekte kjærlighet," he added.

"You said the spell wrong again. Missed some words," Edrym blurted. He had the spell book in his hand. Thorn glowered at him.

"What? I thought you should know," he responded.

"Here it says 'Jeg forbanner deg I morgen attende bursdag å falle ned i et dyp Når en rosetorn skal prikke slikkepott med deg å bli ødelagt av ekte kjærlighet,'" he added.

"I curse you on the morrow of your eighteenth year to fall into a deep sleep when a rose thorn shall prick your finger, to only be broken by true love," Freyah translated.

"I heard him say 'og jeg skaper et band.' I form a bond with you," another mage said.

"Now we know how the bond was formed between you two," Elion replied.

"Since the curse has been fulfilled, fixing the error he made would be of no use," Folmer, another mage, added. He and Thorn used to train together.

"According to the curse, only true love can break it. It's too late, and no magical spell or potion can save her. Only true love," Rhalyf, one of the elders, said. He banged his staff on the ground for emphasis.

"He has dreams of her. There could be a chance of saving her if we found a way to use the dreams somehow to reach her," Edrym suggested.

167

"And do what? Find her a human to fall in love with in the dream world?" Rhalyf chortled.

"Yes. If Thorn can talk to her in his dreams, another human might be able to also," Edrym responded.

Thorn considered the suggestion. The murmurs in the room grew louder as others also discussed the possibilities. It would require trusting a human and working with him. The idea had spun a controversy that left many of the elves arguing.

"Quiet," Elion yelled.

The noise died down after a couple of heartbeats, though a few whispers persisted a bit longer.

"If we were to consider that, what would it entail? Are we to curse another human?" Vasper asked.

"It is utterly unimaginable to try to bind a human to the princess's dream. In all my days, I have never heard of such a thing," Ayre, another elder, replied.

"I agree with Ayre. It has never been done because it is impossible. And true love is rare. How do we even find that one person that she would fall in love with? I heard about her countless rejections of their human lords and princes," Elion said.

"Could the seer help?" asked another.

"It would do no good," said Elion. "Do you forget? Thorn bound her love to the curse. She cannot love another."

"But if she finds love within her dreams while under the curse..."

The discussion continued, and Thorn sighed in relief. No one had proposed that he should attempt to fall in love with the princess since he was the only one who could reach her.

Despite what they hoped, they all knew it would be impossible to link someone else to her now that she was asleep. Now that the curse had taken effect. Finally, the group talked out the matter and came to that very conclusion. It was time to consider other options.

"What if Thorn uses some spell while in the dream? Could that wake her up?" one mage asked.

"The curse is too strong," another replied.

"Or if he gave her the Gyposalia potion in the dream world. It keeps me from sleeping. Maybe it could wake her up," Folmer offered.

"This is a curse, not an ordinary sleep," Freyah replied.

The hall fell silent again. It was a difficult task they had at hand.

"Mages, think. We are the best scholars in Allanar. There must be some way to save the princess and avert war," Elion said.

"Germ Helvola," a voice spoke from the back of the room.

Thorn turned to see who was speaking. It was Elawynn, the daughter of Rhalyf.

"The curse was triggered by a rose thorn pricking the princess's finger," she continued.

"What are you saying?" Elion asked, looking interested.

"She did still have a small bloody wound on her finger," Thorn interjected.

"And the Helvola cures all wounds," Elawynn added.

"No one has seen that plant in years," Vasper said, waving his hand dismissively.

"Yes, because it's a powerful yet rare plant," Rhalyf added, looking at Vasper incredulously. "Anyone who finds one picks it immediately."

"I heard some grow at the western foot of Mount Morend in the Dramnott Kingdom," Elawynn said. An unusual silence fell. That was the heart of the goblin domain.

"Have you forgotten about the creatures that roam Allanar's border? The creatures born of the clash of magic during the war. The journey to Dramnott is dangerous, not to mention Dramnott's the kingdom of our greatest enemies," said Folmer.

"And how sure are we that it will even work?" Ayre asked skeptically.

"Are there any other options? The king has commanded we come up with a cure tonight," Elion said, but no one responded.

"Then it is settled. We will find the Germ Helvola plant and take it to Yeatton."

A knock sounded on the outer door, and two guards entered the council hall. Thorn recognized them from the castle.

"The king requests Mages Elion and Thorn's presence in the throne room," a guard said.

Thorn exhaled deeply as he rose from his seat. Dramnott it was.

"You don't have to go alone," Edrym argued. Thorn folded a clean shirt and a pair of breeches into his brown knapsack.

"Yes, I do. I caused this; I must fix it,"

"Dramnott is far and too dangerous. And there are monsters and ogres in the mountains, too. Let me go with you," Edrym persisted, and Thorn's heart warmed with gratitude. But he must do it alone. No point risking his friend's life or anyone else's for his mistake.

He grabbed his waterskin and hung it around his waist.

"I'll avoid them if I can and fight them when I must. Don't worry about me," Thorn replied. "I'll be fine." He strolled to his reading table to grab the map Elion had given him.

"There must be another way, Thorn." Edrym's voice was full of concern.

"The king insisted that something be done soon. And this is the only way," Thorn responded. The map was torn at its edges, but he could see the paths he had to take to get to Dramnott. He would need to pass through a great deal of wild forest and mountains to reach his destination. No, it would not be easy.

"Here. Have this," Edrym said as he passed his bow and quiver filled with arrows to his friend. He had often bragged about how it was far superior to Thorn's, and the mage appreciated the gesture.

"Thank you," Thorn replied. He hung it on his shoulder and rolled the map into his knapsack.

"Be careful and come back to us."

"I will," he responded.

"Freyah will be mad if you don't," he added. Thorn smiled at the long-running joke.

They walked down the path to the city gates. A few elves greeted him on the way. It seemed that he had redeemed himself in their eyes by volunteering to undertake this quest. Now, if he could only complete it successfully, his life could return to normal.

"Thorn!" Freyah called from behind them. Thorn stopped in his tracks.

"You can't leave without saying goodbye to me first," she said as she wrapped him in a tight hug.

"That's enough already," Edrym said as he pulled the girl away. "He's coming back."

"You have to come back," Freyah insisted.

"I will," Thorn replied.

"Do you plan to sleep on the journey? What if something happens, and you can't wake up?" Edrym asked.

"I will only sleep if I have to. I'm bringing some potions with me to help me stay awake.

Thorn passed through the gateway of the city.

"Be careful, Thorn!" Edrym yelled as his friend advanced into the woods. He wanted nothing more than to accompany him, but he understood. He would've wanted to complete the task alone if it had been him. He would give his friend this chance to clear his name.

The sky was still dark and gloomy. It had been this way since Elora found herself in this strange replica of her world. She stared out the window at the dark clouds, wondering if anything would ever change. Was this it? Was this all she would ever know?

The elf had not been back since the first time they'd met. She was pleased he was not around. She hated him for doing this to her, yet—if she were honest with herself, she would have to admit that she would take his annoying presence over this pervading loneliness. The silence was all-consuming, and the stillness seemed to seep into her bones.

Elora had lost count of how long she had been there. She had tried to keep up with it—those first few hours. But with the sky outside unchanging, no hunger pains demanding she eat, and no weariness begging her to sleep, she had only her internal clock to tell her how time was passing, and the effectiveness of that quickly waned.

For what had to be the hundredth time, she wandered the halls, following the path the elf had discovered when he was there. As she walked, she made a decision. There was no use bemoaning her fate. If this were to be where she would spend the rest of her life, she would make the best of it.

She would still explore any means of escape. She wouldn't accept this fate lightly. But she would also attempt to find ways to make her existence here as bearable as possible.

Elora shivered and crossed her arms, hugging herself tightly as a shadow seemed to move to her right. She watched it slither across the wall. She backed away slowly until it disappeared around a corner.

What was in here with her? She ran back to her chamber, slammed the door, and locked it. Backing farther into the room, she climbed on her bed, huddled against the backboard. Where had that elf sent her?

Thorn gazed around the streets. The castle stood to his right, and the city's gates opened a mile to his left. He

could see the gap in the wall from where he stood. This was where the dream had first deposited him the last time until he had closed his eyes and been transported inside.

He turned his back on the castle and headed to the wall. So, if he didn't enter the castle, he could move around freely. Or would there be boundaries here, too? He began to feel the resistance after he had only gone a few feet as if the air itself thickened to push him back. It grew unbearable after only a few steps more, yet still, he resisted. He would make it home, and barring that, he would at least make it out of this blasted city.

But it was no use. Almost immediately, his body met an irresistible barrier. Everywhere around, his way was blocked. Everywhere except back. He struggled against it for a long time, but all in vain. Finally, he gave in to the inevitable. He turned and headed to the castle.

Elora was disgusted with herself. She had always been proud of her courage and willingness to take on any challenge, no matter how dangerous, and here she was, cowering on her bed because of a shadow.

What could a shadow do to her? It wasn't as if it could kill her, even if it could touch her. And so what if it could? Wouldn't that be preferable to this infernal existence?

She scooted off her bed and grabbed the poker from the fireplace. She stared at its shadowy flames before shaking her head and moving to the door. This was her world now, strange as it might be. She wouldn't let anything keep her from doing what she wanted here.

She held the poker high as she marched from her chambers. She would go to the library and read for a while. At least she had that entertainment open to her.

She glided down the hallway, her slippers making no noise against the stone floor. This time, she made it to the castle entrance before she saw anything. But then, there it was. A shadow moving against the wall in the foyer. She hid herself at the mouth of the passage and waited in the darkness as it came closer. She held her poker high over her head, ready for an attack.

She didn't have to wait long before a tall shape rounded the corner. She squeezed her eyes shut and brought the poker down with all the force she could muster. Something stopped its descent too early.

Her eyes jerked open to see the elf standing there, a hateful glare on his face, his hand on the poker where he had grabbed it before it came crashing into his skull. She let out a cry as he ripped it from her hands and threw it to the floor. Without a word, he walked past her down the hallway.

She knew she should let him go. She shouldn't give him the satisfaction of knowing how desperately lonely she was.

But she was desperately lonely.

Oh, so desperately lonely.

She couldn't stop herself. She hastily retrieved the poker and scurried after him. She stared at his back as they walked and tried to imagine that it was Adrian she followed. Maybe it wasn't too late to try to love him. Maybe he could still break her curse if she succeeded.

But no. She knew the man well enough. He would have been one of the first to try. He had already failed, and his failure would have driven him away long ago.

175

But still, his company would be vastly preferable to the elf's, so she reached into her imagination and pictured him walking in front of her. The elf was too tall, so she imagined him shorter. His shoulders were too broad, so she imagined them narrower. The muscles she could see bulging through his shirt appeared too firm, so she imagined them weaker.

Hmm, she thought. Adrian isn't doing well in this comparison. But it wasn't appearance that mattered when choosing a friend. It was their personality, and despite what others thought, she liked Adrian's personality, so she continued. She shortened the long brown hair in her mind and rounded the pointed ears.

Suddenly, she gasped, and the elf turned to face her.

No, Adrian turned to face her.

"Adrian?"

"What do you want?" The voice wasn't right. It was too deep, too gravelly. That's alright. She could change that, too. She didn't know how she knew. She just knew.

She walked up to the man waiting before her with a puzzled expression. She reached out and tentatively touched the soft skin of his face. No, that wasn't right either. Adrian had rougher skin. She touched him again. Yes, that was better.

"Adrian, is it really you?"

"You've gone mad, woman," Adrian said, jerking away from her. Suddenly, he was gone, and the elf stood in his place.

"What did you do?!"

Wrinkles formed on his forehead, and he turned his head slightly, gazing at her askance. "I did nothing."

His voice was still his, stone rubbing against stone. "What did you see?"

She crossed her arms and scowled, pressing her lips together tightly.

"Tell me, human. The more I can learn about this place, the sooner I can escape this predicament."

She scoffed. "Why should I help you?"

He locked his eyes with hers. "Because I'm trying to help you."

Elora rolled her eyes. "Of course you are. Why wouldn't you? It's not like you're the one who put me here in the first place."

Thorn hesitated. He didn't want to tell her. It felt too much like admitting defeat. But even if he managed to find the plant and get it to her. And even if it cured her. He didn't know how it would affect him. Would their bond pull him out of the curse, too, or would he still have to face this strange land whenever he fell asleep?

He needed to know as much as he could, and if telling her his mission was what it took to make her talk, he would have to swallow his pride and do so. But it still rankled.

"I am, actually," he said. "Your father has threatened war if I don't find a way to awaken you, and my people would prefer not to start another war at this time."

Elora stared at him. He seemed to be telling the truth. She burst out laughing. "Oh, father," she said, looking around, "I should have known you wouldn't give up on me." A smile spread across her face. However, it wavered a bit. "I thought elf magic was too powerful. I thought you couldn't break a curse once it had been cast except by fulfilling its requirements."

"That's true, but there's a plant, Helvola. It is said to be able to cure all wounds. He grabbed her hand and held it in front of her face. We are hoping that if it is used to cure this wound," he nodded at her finger and the drop of blood that still pooled there, "it will break the curse."

"Is that possible?" she asked, staring at her finger.

Thorn threw her hand away. "We can only try. Now, tell me what you saw."

"Wait a minute," protested Elora. "Are you bringing the plant to me now? What is happening in the real world? When will you try this cure?"

Thorn huffed. "I don't have it yet. I'm on a quest to find it as we speak."

"Oh, how long will it take?"

"If I survive and all goes well, I should have it in a week."

Elora bit her bottom lip. She picked at a loose thread dangling from her sleeve. "Will you visit me each night and tell me how things are going?

The elf growled at her and turned away, but he didn't leave. "Very well," he said. "Now," he faced her again, "tell me what you saw."

"I saw my friend, Adrian."

"Yes, I'm familiar with the man. How did this happen? Are you delirious?"

"No, I'm not delirious! I was just thinking how frustrating it was that I was so lonely. Even your company was a welcome change."

He frowned.

"Then, I wished you were Adrian. I thought that if I couldn't have him here, I could at least pretend. So, I remembered how he looked and imagined that you were *him. As I pictured the differences between the two of you, the changes I made in my mind actually happened. You looked just like him."*

Thorn carefully considered her words. "Try it again."

She nodded and stared at him intently.

He pushed her back. "Not on me. Try it on something else." He pointed to a nearby chair. "Change that chair."

"To what?"

"To a desk."

Elora focused on the chair, imagining it wider and taller. She pictured the cushioned seat changing into a flat marble surface. The legs darker and stouter. As she imagined, so it became. Before their eyes, the seat morphed into a tall, elegant desk.

"Interesting," said Thorn. "It seems you can control this dream world of yours. I wonder..." Before he could say any more, he suddenly vanished.

Elora whimpered in despair at his absence. He must have woken up. She was alone again.

Chapter 12

Thorn awoke with a start as a fox ran into the brush nearby. It must have been the animal who startled him from his slumber. He sat up and ran his hands through his long hair, looking around to get his bearings. He was back.

He pulled out the map from his knapsack. The path through the trees before him was the way to Mount Morend.

The way to a forest full of magical creatures of the dark.

The way to goblin strongholds.

The way he must go if he wanted to save his people.

He sighed as he returned the map and pushed himself to his feet. The forest grew thick around him. The path visible only to those familiar with the ways of the wild.

Thorn ignored the grumbling of his stomach as he made his way through the dense underbrush. He would stop to eat soon, but he wanted to make as much headway as he could first. He couldn't complete this mission quickly enough.

Strange sounds filled the air as he strolled deeper into the trees. Thorn stopped and listened. He was sure he had heard something in the distance—an unusual sound, something that didn't belong in a typical forest.

The whispering leaves, the gentle murmur of a nearby stream—all fell silent. Magic.

He scanned the towering trees and felt a sudden shift in the air, a palpable sense of tension that raised the hairs on his arms. His keen elven senses told him that danger was approaching swiftly. As he cautiously continued along the winding forest path, the towering trees seemed to close in around him, their branches casting eerie, shifting shadows.

The air was heavy with enchantment, and the magical energy was palpable. The unsettling noise grew louder. It was a guttural growl, a sound that emanated from something far more sinister than any woodland creature he knew.

The mage's hand instinctively went to the hilt of his sword, ready to summon the elements at a moment's notice. Thorn walked in silence, his eyes scanning the underbrush for any sign of movement. It wasn't long before he sensed a presence, an unsettling feeling that something was watching him from the shadows.

Then it emerged—a creature that defied description. Towering above him, it was a monstrous fusion of beast and magic, a creature born of the forest's enchantments. A monster of nightmarish proportions—a massive, hulking beast with dark, mottled fur that seemed to absorb the moonlight.

Its fur shimmered with an otherworldly glow, patterns of bioluminescent runes etched into its hide. Its eyes, two swirling orbs of violet and green, held an eerie intelligence that sent a shiver down Thorn's spine.

The creature's head was adorned with a crown of jagged, twisting horns, each as long as a man's arm. Its mighty limbs ended in enormous claws that could easily

181

rend flesh from bone. Saliva dripped from its gaping maw, sizzling as it hit the forest floor, dissolving leaves and twigs wherever it fell.

The creature's growl grew louder, reverberating through the forest like a distant thunderstorm. It stalked toward Thorn, its massive form casting a shadow that blotted out the light. In one swift, fluid motion, the elf drew his sword, and with a deep breath, Thorn channeled his magic, summoning the power of the elements. Flames flickered to life along the blade, casting a warm, orange glow over the surrounding trees. The earth beneath his feet trembled as he called forth its strength.

Unimpressed by Thorn's display of power, the creature lunged with startling speed. Its claws, sharp as obsidian, swiped through the air, seeking to tear the man to pieces. Thorn parried the attack with his sword, the clash of elements sparking and sizzling as their forces collided. The impact sent shockwaves through his arms, and he gritted his teeth against the pain.

The monster, a grotesque embodiment of the forest's malevolence, moved with surprising agility for its colossal size. Each swipe of its massive claws was like a falling tree, a tremendous force. The ground trembled beneath their feet.

Thorn's elven agility and mastery over the elements were his greatest assets in this brutal dance of life and death. He parried the creature's attacks gracefully, his sword blazing with elemental fire. With every clash of metal on iron-tough flesh, sparks flew, illuminating the darkness of the forest.

However, the mage's body bore the brunt of the beast's ferocious attacks. His limbs ached from the relentless battering, and every impact threatened to shatter his bones. Each swipe of the monster's claws left deep gouges in his leather armor, now ripped and battered from the many strikes it had absorbed.

The creature's movements were a blur, and Thorn found himself hard-pressed to defend against the relentless assault. His magical barriers strained under the onslaught, and his swordsmanship was pushed to its limits.

With every blow he landed on the creature, Thorn could feel his strength waning. It was as though the forest itself conspired to sap his vitality as if the monster drew power from the very trees that surrounded them. His breath grew ragged, and beads of sweat mingled with the dirt and grime on his face.

Yet, he refused to relent. Thorn's determination burned brighter than the flames he summoned.

Drawing upon his elemental powers, he called forth a vortex of wind, sending leaves and debris swirling around him. The creature faltered for a moment, disoriented by the sudden gale. It was the opening Thorn needed.

With a precise strike, he drove his blade into the creature's flank, where its magical defenses were weakest. A howl of pain and rage echoed through the forest as the monster staggered back, its form flickering like a failing illusion.

Thorn did not relent. With another surge of magic, he conjured a torrent of flames that engulfed the creature. Finally, with a final, powerful strike, Thorn drove his blade into the beast's heart.

A brilliant explosion of fire and wind erupted, sending the creature crashing to the forest floor with an earth-shattering roar. Its form flickering and fading like a ghostly apparition, the monster's howls of agony filled the night. Weakened and scorched, it finally dissipated into a cloud of fading magic, leaving only a smoky, iridescent residue behind.

Thorn stood there, chest heaving, the echoes of the battle fading away. He was injured, his clothes torn, but he was still alive. He fell to his knees and took deep, steadying breaths, pushing down the pain.

He was an elf. His wounds would quickly heal, but he might not reach his destination in one piece if he ran into many more such creatures. With renewed resolve, he rose to his feet and set off deeper into this forbidden, enchanted forest.

Thorn tore off the rags that were all that remained of his shirt. He ripped apart a small section of fabric and dipped it into the stream. He washed off the blood and gore that covered his chest, wincing as the cloth passed over his wounds. He bandaged the worst cuts using strips of his ruined garment. The others would heal quickly enough on their own.

With a grunt of pain, he fed another log onto the fire and bit into some dried jerky. The deep, rich, salty taste danced around his mouth, and the strong, smoky aroma blended well with the campfire.

He had fought two more creatures since he'd defeated the first one. And his body was covered in cuts and bruises. This, though, this felt heavenly. The food couldn't compare to a home-cooked elven meal, but in his current state, it was ambrosia.

He had planned to sleep as little as he could on this journey, but his body needed the rest to heal efficiently. And he wanted to see what else he could discover about the cursed world.

He pulled on his elemental magic and set fire to the ring that he had cleared all around him. With his magic imbued in it, it would burn all night. And since those creatures feared fire, he should be safe to rest here, uncomfortably warm as it might be. In no time, he was fast asleep.

He walked into the castle and searched the corridors and rooms for the human. He wanted to discover more about her ability to control this strange place. He finally found her in the library, curled up before a hazy fire, reading a book.

Her face lit up slightly when she saw him, then fell instantly, as if it realized how it had betrayed her.

She mumbled something that might be taken for a greeting, then returned to reading her book.

That was fine. He would experiment himself if she weren't in the mood to help him. He turned and walked out of the room. He would go back to the entrance. If he had the same ability as she did to change things here, perhaps he could change one of the boundaries. A smirk crossed his face when he heard her light footsteps fall in behind him.

When he reached the foyer, he swung open the tall double doors and stepped outside. He immediately found himself in the upstairs corridor. He made his way back to the entry and saw the princess sitting on the floor by the grand staircase, leaning against the wall. She didn't comment, and neither did he.

He opened the door again. This time, before he stepped through, he reached for his magic. He could barely sense it deep within. It passed through his mental hand like smoke whenever he tried to grab it. Very well, then. He would try another tactic. Following the human's example, he used his imagination.

He imagined the foyer where he stood being on the other side of the doorway. He pictured it clearly in his mind until the image of the courtyard shimmied and changed. With a satisfied nod, he stepped through the opening. And found himself in the upstairs corridor.

Thorn slammed his fist into a wooden doorpost, cracking and splintering the structure and sending a new wave of pain down his arm.

Once again, he thought as he headed back down the stairs.

She had to admire his persistence. And his physique. That stray thought popped unbidden into her head, and she quickly pushed it away.

What did the man mean by coming to her dream castle without a shirt? Didn't he realize how indecent it was? How scandalous he looked? He probably didn't care. You would think that elves had better manners than that.

Elora shifted her position on the floor. Her bootie had grown sore from sitting on the hard stone for so long. She watched the elf standing in the middle of the room, staring ferociously at the open doorway.

She understood what he was trying to do. She was curious as well. Could he shift the barriers? Suddenly, she saw the moving shadow again. It had appeared and disappeared with increasing frequency since she first perceived it. She jumped to her feet and grabbed Thorn's arm.

"Elf," she said, pulling at him. The frustrating thing didn't move a step. He just glared down at her.

"Unhand me, human." He jerked his arm out of her grasp.

"Fine. Get yourself killed. I don't care." She turned and ran from the room.

Thorn watched her go curiously. Then shrugged and regained his focus on the door. When the image of the foyer was the clearest it had yet been, he stepped through the opening. But just a split second before his foot landed, he felt a rush of wind blow across his back as if a mighty force had struck at him and only just missed.

His surroundings faded, and he found himself again in the upper corridor. What was that? His experiments forgotten, he set off in search of the princess. He found her, with poker in hand once again, back in the library.

"What was that?" he demanded.

The girl ignored him. He rubbed his hand over his face in frustration. He had to learn about this place, and his best chance of gaining information seemed to be with the infernal being sitting before him. He had to find some way to get her to cooperate.

He walked over and sat down in the chair opposite her own. For a while, he just watched her read. He searched for her emotions in the stillness of the room, but he couldn't feel them. Not even sporadically as he had that first time. They were as silent as everything else in this strange place.

She began fidgeting under his gaze, and he allowed himself an evil grin. Then he remembered he needed to make peace with her.

"What is your name?" he barked.

She raised her head and glared at him. "Why do you care?"

"I don't, but it is awkward calling you 'human' all the time."

She sat in silence for a long time. He waited quietly and watched her. Her eyes strayed to the fireplace, then back to him, resting first on his naked, bandaged chest, then shooting quickly to his face as a blush painted her cheeks a slightly darker gray.

For a brief moment, he wondered what she would look like in the real world. In full color. She was beautiful here. How much more so would she be with the colors of her hair, her eyes, her skin on display?

The blush didn't fade from her cheeks as she looked back at her book and answered him abruptly. "Elora."

That was interesting. Her embarrassment at the sight of his bare chest could only indicate attraction. He might be able to use that to get her to cooperate.

"Greetings, Elora. I am Thorn." He held out his hand in a gesture of peace, but she made no move toward it.

"I hate you," she mumbled as she continued pretending to read her book.

"And I hate you."

Elora raised her head to shoot him a scalding glare before returning her gaze to the tome in her lap.

"But we have a mutual problem here. I propose a temporary truce."

"I'm listening."

"I need to know as much about this place as you can tell me and as I can discover. The more I know, the more likely I'll be able to find a way to break us free from its hold."

"I thought the plant was supposed to free me."

"I'm hoping it will."

"So, your people don't face a war," she said with a smirk.

He frowned. "I'm hoping it will," he repeated forcefully. "But there's no guarantee. If it doesn't work, we'll need to pursue other options. The sooner we can find those options, the better."

Elora sighed. She closed her book and set it on the table beside her.

"What do you want to know?"

"First, what was that in the foyer?"

Elora shrugged. "I don't know, but I've been seeing it around more frequently as of late. It has a terrifyingly menacing presence. I sense evil all around it."

"Has it ever attacked you?"

"No, I've managed to avoid it so far, but, I don't know, I feel that if it did get ahold of me... Well, I avoid it, and I suggest you do, too."

"Alright. We will avoid the shadow."

The easy way he dismissed the threat seemed to rankle her, but he didn't care. "Have you experimented any more with your imagination?"

"Yes." She pulled her legs up on the chair, crossing them under her. Not a very princess-like pose, but she was only a human, after all.

189

"What were the results?" he asked through gritted teeth. Did the annoying woman not see the urgency of their situation? He would kill her if he had to spend much more time here with only her company.

Could he kill her here? His hands itched to try, but such an attempt wouldn't further his cause.

"I can change anything now, but it doesn't last very long."

"Have you tried the boundaries?"

"No."

Of course, she hadn't. The stupid human had probably focused on changing her clothes or the tapestries, not anything useful.

"Let me see what you can do."

"Please," she said, reminding him of his manners.

"Please," he forced out, his lip rising in a snarl.

Elora turned her attention to the table where her book rested. She concentrated, and Thorn watched as it transformed into a lovely fountain. A bowl sat at the top, spilling water into the marble basin beneath. Droplets escaped from its containment and splashed on Thorn's pants.

"How long can you hold it?" he asked as he leaned forward and trailed his hand through the water.

Her eyes squinted with the strain of the effort. Finally, she released it with a gasp, and the fountain regained its original form, albeit a bit wetter than it had begun.

"Keep practicing," he said as he felt himself begin to fade.

"You're not my master," she replied heatedly.

"I thought we had a truce."

"A truce doesn't mean you tell me what to do."

"Fine. Where do you think we should go from here?"

"I'll keep practicing," she said, wrinkling her cute nose at him.

"Good. You do that." He tore his eyes from her bewitching face and let himself wake.

Goblins Vrek, Bral, and Briq sat huddled over their drinks in the barrack's dining hall. Human soldiers meandered around them, but no one gave them a second glance. That was because they didn't look like goblins Vrek, Bral, and Briq. They looked like young humans, new recruits, to be more precise. They sat near the officer's table, and officers never paid any attention to new recruits unless they got in their way.

The officers kept their voices low as they discussed kingdom business, but goblins, like elves, had excellent hearing. Even in these forms, they had no trouble following their entire conversation.

"The king has given the elves one more week. He said we'll attack if they don't produce the mage by then. He started moving some platoons into position last week," one of the officers told another who had been away on assignment.

"But that's madness! How can we survive a war against the elves?" he replied.

"He believes their war with the goblins weakened them and drained their resources. Why else would they be willing to give in to our demands? Minister Thorton reported that they sent someone on a quest to retrieve a magical plant that might be able to wake her. That's a great deal of effort to appease someone you don't feel threatened by."

The first officer rubbed his scruffy beard. "Can he make it back by the deadline?"

"They believe so. All he has to do is get to the plant. He can magic himself back here after that."

"So, the one seeking the plant is the mage that cursed her then?"

"Why do you think so?"

"Captain Jarden said that they can only magic themselves somewhere they've already been. He's the only one that has been here, isn't he?"

"Whoever it is, we must hope they succeed. The threat of war goes a long way, but an actual war would do nothing to help our princess or our kingdom."

"I guess we'll know one way or another in a week's time."

Vrek motioned to the other two, and they quietly left their seats and hurried back to their headquarters in the basement of the castle.

"What are we going to do?" asked Bral when the door had closed behind them. "If we don't act quickly, the elves may find a cure, and all our planning will have been in vain."

"We can't act yet," argued Briq. "The king and queen and her friends still sit with her. She's never alone. We can't risk hurting one of them, especially not the king or queen."

"Why not?" asked Bral. "Wouldn't that make our success even greater? If elves kill not only the princess but the queen, too..."

"No," said Vrek. "The king must live as must the queen." He looked Bral straight in the eyes. "The king is the one who will make the decision to support us. If he dies, another will take his place, and we have no way of knowing what he will do.

The queen must live because she is the most emotional of the two. If the king's logic sways him from our cause, the queen's emotion will pull him back. As for her friends," he said callously, "they can die. Unfortunately, they keep to no schedule. There is no way to know who will be sitting with her when or for how long. We cannot risk arriving when the king or queen is there. We will need to wait a little longer."

"But what if the elves return with a cure before we get our chance?" argued Bral.

"We'll just have to keep an eye on the situation," said Briq.

"In the meantime," said Vrek with an evil glint in his eyes, "I'll have a talk with the king. It's about time I tried some more remedies, and he needs to hear how untrustworthy and deceptive the elves really are. When I get through with him, he won't let them anywhere near the castle, even if they bring her true love to him on a platter."

With wicked grins on their faces, the three went through the inner door and joined their men.

Thorn lay down reluctantly that night. The day had been relatively uneventful, just a few skirmishes, a ferocious cat as tall as he was, a bear with claws the length of his arm, nothing he couldn't easily handle. His old wounds had healed already, and his new ones were minor. He wanted to continue the journey. He debated whether he should. If the cure didn't work, he would have ample time to explore the dream world later.

However, something seemed to pull him back there. He glanced at the stars overhead. He still had plenty of time to complete his mission, and Cascading Falls was only five or six hours from his current location. It would be easier to tackle that challenge fully rested in the light of day. With these logical reasons in mind, he lay down and fell asleep.

Thorn blinked rapidly when he walked into the castle. Everything was different. Some color and light had even appeared. Not much. The world was still awash in shades of gray, but the slightest hints of reds and blues could be seen if a person looked closely enough. And the entire castle appeared just a bit brighter, less gloomy.

The princess was waiting for him. She sat on the bottom step of the grand staircase. She seemed to be trying to control the smile that appeared in danger of breaking out on her face.

Impressive, he thought. The girl was strong. He had to admire her courage and determination in the face of the likelihood of a lifetime in this place. Even if he hated her, he couldn't deny that.

He glowered at her to remind her they weren't friends, and all semblance of a smile vanished. Instead, her head tilted up, nose in the air. He could almost envision fur and whiskers on her face, so like an enraged kitten, she appeared.

"I've figured out how to make the changes permanent," she said with a sniff.

"Good. You can help me try to break through the boundaries on the front doors."

"Why?"

"Why?!" he asked incredulously. "So, we can get out of the castle, you infuriating human."

"It's Elora. Didn't you ask my name so you wouldn't have to call me human anymore?"

Thorn growled then gritted his teeth. "Very well, Elora. We need to break through the barriers so we can get out of the castle."

"Why do we need to get out of the castle?"

Thorn stared at her, stunned. He didn't know. Now that he thought about it, he wasn't sure. At first, he'd wanted to find a way to return to the elven lands, but now that he knew he wasn't trapped here, that was no longer a priority. But they did need to find a way out of the castle. He felt that truth all the way to his bones, even if he didn't understand why.

"I'm not sure, but I know we do. Besides, if we can break through the boundaries, that should weaken the curse, if nothing else."

"Alright," Elora agreed reluctantly. She stared intently at the open doorway, and in no time, a mirror image of the foyer appeared on the other side.

Thorn stepped through. And found himself in the upstairs corridor. He took a deep breath and headed back downstairs.

They tried several more times, and the image grew stronger each time, but it didn't matter. Even with the vision appearing completely solid, he still ended up in the corridor.

"We need to try something else," he said.

Elora sat on the bottom step of the staircase, fiddling with the fireplace poker she always had on hand.

"What do you suggest?"

"Instead of redirecting it, let's see if we can break it completely."

Elora rose and walked over to him, laying the poker down beside the door. She tilted her head and studied the open doorway. "How can we do that?"

"Try imagining it as a rock wall. If you succeed in transforming it, I can break it down."

"Shouldn't we try something less solid, like a wooden wall? It would be easier to break through."

"No. In order for it to work, the wall would have to match the strength of the boundary. Otherwise, some of the magical boundary might remain even after the wall is gone."

"Very well then, a rock wall." Elora focused on the doorway again, this time looking at the barely visible shimmer of magic instead of through it. It didn't transform as quickly this time.

Thorn stepped up beside her and delved into the depths of his own imagination to help. Together, they managed a weak, thin phantom of a wall. But it wasn't enough.

"I have an idea," he said. "Let me into your mind. If I can link with your thoughts directly, we will have a better chance of accomplishing this."

"What do you mean let you into my mind?" Elora took a step back, her eyes wide with horror.

"Let me into your mind. What is it about that that you don't understand."

"I'm not letting you in my mind!"

"Look, human."

Elora glared at him.

196

"Elora. Look, Elora. You have the imagination to do what we need but not the strength. I have the strength but not the imagination. If I can link with your mind, I can lend you my strength. We may succeed."

She gazed at him skeptically.

"If we don't," he insisted, "there's no way we'll ever get through."

Elora thought that was a bit dramatic, but she did see his point.

"Will this be like the bond we had before?"

"Yes, but a little stronger since I'm making the link directly."

"Very well. What do I need to do?"

"Just stand still." He moved up behind her and wrapped his arms around her. She fought him, trying to shake him off.

He released her, and she whipped around to face him.

"What are you doing?!"

"Don't flatter yourself, hum—Elora. I don't relish this any more than you do, but I have to be close to you to make the link. It requires physical contact. The closer we are, the stronger it will be."

Elora turned her back to him again. "Fine! Just get it over with."

Thorn wrapped her in his arms and held her tightly. He rested his chin on the top of her head, closed his eyes, and sunk into her mind. She smelled nice, he thought before forcing his thoughts back to the task at hand.

A flood of emotions rushed through him, so much stronger than their previous bond caused. His direct connection to her mind gave him infinitely more access. He couldn't resist exploring.

Surprisingly, fear was the greatest emotion. He had expected it to be hatred or disgust. Did she fear him? The thought didn't give him as much pleasure as it should.

There was also something else there, so close to the surface. And it wasn't disgust. He tightened his arms around her experimentally. Yes, she was attracted to him, quite a bit actually, and his touch was doing fascinating things to her body. He smirked. Interesting. She squirmed against his tight hold, and his body responded.

He jerked his mind away from those dangerous emotions and focused on her hate. The intensity of it helped him remember his and the reason they were in their current position.

"Now," he said. "Picture the door as a solid wall."

The image formed in her mind, and he latched onto it, feeding it, expanding it. He directed the few trickles of his magic that he could reach into the vision. And it slowly began to form. He instinctively held her tighter as their minds merged more intensely. It worked. A wall had replaced the boundary.

They stood there, their breaths coming fast and heavy. Her body molded to his. He found himself reluctant to release her, and she didn't break away. So they remained, much longer than was necessary. With his mind still linked to hers, he felt the emotions swirling through her. Hatred and desire. It wouldn't take much, he thought, to tip the scales in the more favorable direction. No!

He pushed her away, breaking the connection, and walked over to the wall. He didn't want that. It didn't matter how beautiful she was. She was the enemy. He shoved the rebellious thoughts out of his head and forced his body under control.

Reaching up, he ran his hand over the wall. He didn't look at Elora when she joined him, but he could tell she was angry. Her rage radiated off her in waves that his elven senses easily felt. His abrupt release of her might have made her angry, but he was willing to bet she would have been even more furious if he hadn't let her go.

If he had explored other possibilities.

After the emotions had died down, and it was done, she would never forgive herself for giving in to an enemy in such a way. She didn't realize how close to danger she had been.

Thorn picked up the fireplace poker from where Elora had dropped it and tested the wall's strength. Completely solid. Good. He used the tip of the poker to chip away at the mortar between the stones.

Chapter 13

E lora sat on the stairs and watched him until he faded away, and the fireplace poker fell to the floor with a clang. She hugged herself when she was once again alone. She tried imagining him back but only managed to produce a thin apparition. She made the phantom hold a ghost fireplace poker and work on the wall. No sound accompanied its efforts, and no dust scattered in the air, but it was comforting all the same.

Was she going crazy that she found comfort in a vision of her enemy? She remembered how it had felt when he stood behind her, his hard body pressed so intimately against her own. A shiver shook her frame, and emotions she would rather not feel rushed to the surface. He had been in her head. Had he sensed her feelings? Did he know what he did to her?

She cringed at the thought, then set her mouth stubbornly. Well, so what if he did? Surely, he knew how handsome he was. Anyone who looked like that couldn't not be aware of it. And it was only natural that her body reacted the way it did. It had nothing to do with what she thought. If he could sense those unwelcome emotions, then he could also sense how much she despised him.

Yes, he was smart enough to understand. He was a very intelligent man; she'd give him that. Despite everything else, he was intelligent.

And strong.

She remembered the feel of his muscular arms holding her so tightly. And he had smelled perfect. Like pine and fire. Wild and powerful.

Elora shook those thoughts out of her head. She walked over to the wall and picked up the metal tool. She began scrapping away between the stones. She'd have some of the work, if not all, done before he returned. She'd show him that this human wasn't helpless without him.

Thorn emerged from the forest and stood at the edge of the Serpentine River. Only about two or two and a half days left before he would reach Mount Morend. A few yards away, Cascading Falls spilled its water into the rushing torrents. The sunlight glittered off the falling water like diamonds, and rainbows cast their glow around it. He would have to climb the cliffs beside the waterfall to reach the cave tunnel, his only safe path to his destination.

As Thorn studied the rushing current he would need to cross, the roar of the falls almost made him miss the rustle of leaves behind him. He whipped around, sword in his hand, and waited.

Surprise filled him as the human, Adrian, emerged from the trees covered in cuts and bruises, his hair ruffled, his clothing torn. He looked exactly as he should if he had encountered even one-fourth of the problems Thorn had. He had probably come through Glarendell Pass and missed the best action. Mores the pity.

"What are you doing here?" he asked the human.

"Looking for you. I'm hoping to cash in that favor you owe me."

Of all the strange things Thorn had encountered on his journey, this was the strangest.

"Now?"

"If you would be so kind."

Thorn returned his sword to its scabbard and crossed his arms. "Very well, what can I do to repay the favor?"

"I want you to enchant an item with your sleeping curse."

"You do not want to force me to awaken the princess?"

Adrian glared down at his feet. "No. That's all in the past now. She will have to endure the end she has chosen. So, what do you say? Will you do it?

"No."

"Why not?" Adrian asked, visibly rattled. "I did save your life after all."

Thorn scoffed. "Perhaps. Though the small group that waited for us would have posed no real challenge."

"They might have taken down a few of you before you realized they were there."

"It's not likely." He breathed deeply, the crisp scent of the river washing over him. "I will not lightly subject another to the fate I visited on the princess, especially someone I do not know. What else would you ask for?"

"Give me the words of the curse then."

"Your human mages would not be able to cast it. It's an elven curse."

"Then what can be the harm?"

Thorn considered his request. "Very well," he agreed. With a few modifications, he thought to himself. "Do you have parchment, pen, and ink?"

Adrian hurriedly removed his pack and rummaged around for the requested items.

Thorn copied down the curse. However, he changed it so that anyone who fell under it would only sleep for a hundred years instead of for all eternity.

Also, he put no restrictions on their ability to love, and he put in a safeguard so that it wouldn't be effective against an elf. If some human did somehow miraculously manage to enact the curse, their victim would have a better chance of escaping it.

And if things went well that night, there might not be a cursed world for anyone to be sent to, thereby making the entire thing superfluous. He handed the parchment to Adrian.

"Is that it? Are we even now?"

Adrian waved it around to dry it, folded it carefully, and repacked his bag.

"Yes, I think that will do it. It was a pleasure doing business with you." The man held out his hand to Thorn.

Thorn recrossed his arms and narrowed his eyes at him.

"Then, perhaps you should return to your kingdom."

"Yes," said Adrian, backing away hastily. "I think I'll do that." He turned and disappeared back the way he had come. It was only then that Thorn wondered how he had found him. He would think on the matter another day. Now, he had to make his way up the falls.

Chuckling to himself at the strangeness of it all, Thorn walked toward the river. Water magic was not his strongest power, but he could control it enough to manage this. As he approached the bank, the air grew thick with magical energy, and unusual ripples began forming on the water's surface. Ripples that went against the normal current.

From the depths emerged a creature unlike any he had ever seen, a being born of pure magic. A water serpent with glistening scales, its eyes gleamed with an otherworldly intelligence.

Its body coiled beneath the surface, and without hesitation, the serpent lunged, its form blurring as it moved with incredible speed. Thorn narrowly avoided its attack, feeling the rush of displaced air as it passed. Clearly, his usual weapons and spells would be of little use alone against an opponent composed entirely of water. He would have to think of something else.

The serpent continued its relentless assault, striking with liquid fangs and attempting to ensnare him in its watery coils. Thorn's agile form proved his greatest asset as he evaded each attack, his reflexes pushed to their limits.

He realized that brute force alone would not suffice either. He began to move, fluid and graceful, as if performing an intricate dance. With each step, he called upon his mastery of the elements.

His magic flowed through him as he summoned a tempestuous gust of wind that swirled around the river. The air currents disrupted the water serpent's form, causing it to momentarily lose cohesion. It thrashed and roared in frustration.

Seizing the opportunity, Thorn focused his magic further, drawing energy from the earth beneath his feet. The ground quivered with his command as a series of crystalline spikes erupted from the earth. They formed a protective barrier, encircling him and keeping the creature at bay.

The serpent surged against this newfound obstacle, its body struggling to reform. But Thorn's elemental mastery held firm.

With a final surge of magic, he summoned a torrential downpour from the sky. Rain cascaded into the glade, drenching the water serpent and further destabilizing its form.

Rainwater mixed with the magic river water that made up the creature's being. The serpent appeared to melt as the rainwater ran down its length, refusing to meld with the magic and further disrupting its stability. The snake writhed and sputtered, unable to maintain its attack.

Thorn didn't hesitate. Drawing his sword, he leaped forward, his blade cutting through the watery being's core. With a shimmering burst of liquid, the serpent dissipated into a fine mist, mingling with the rain.

Breathing heavily, Thorn sheathed his sword and stood before the now-calm river. He stepped into the wide stream, forming the water into a platform beneath his feet. In this manner, he approached the waterfall.

He had to raise a wind shield before him to keep the force of the water from knocking him into the churning liquid at the base of the falls. His shirt stuck to him like a second skin, the cold wetness of it quite uncomfortable. Yet, he was still glad he had packed this extra one since his other had been lost. After this climb, he might need some more bandages.

He adjusted his pack and sword and reached up to find a handhold. The rock was slimy and slick. More than once, he lost his hold and fell into the water below. After the first fall, he tried to form an air platform to carry him up, but the force of the water was too great for him to maintain it.

He tried banishing the water from where he needed to climb, but there was too much rushing too quickly for it to do any good. In the end, all he could do was climb.

Hours later, he reached the cave behind the waterfall, scratched and bruised. He moved farther back into its dark recesses. He had brought no provisions for a fire. It wouldn't have been any good if he had. They would only have hampered his ascent, and by the time he'd arrived at the cave, they would be too wet to light. Even if he had magically removed the water from them, the cave was too damp.

But he needed to get dry. He removed his clothes and hung them over a stalagmite. He summoned a small fire in the palm of his hand since that was the only way he could keep it going without something to burn. Calling forth a small wind behind him, he directed it past the fire and toward the clothes. The warm air it generated would dry them quickly enough, and the fire in his hand would warm him.

He would eat something and then sleep there that night. In the morning, he would venture into the heart of the mountain.

Elora once again stood before the wall, chipping away at the mortar. She had taken a break earlier, but not because she had to. She didn't feel any hunger or tiredness here. Her hand wasn't even sore from all the work. She had gotten bored. That was all.

Elora felt relatively comfortable in this strange place now. She had managed to bring some color to most of it—mainly the places she frequented. And there was less gloom and despair in the atmosphere. And in herself. She still wanted to wake up. Badly. But the thought of a future here didn't terrify her like it had. As long as Thorn continued to visit.

She frowned at the thought. She still hated the man. Handsome and compelling, though he might be. It didn't matter that the idea of him made her tingle inside. He was an elf, and he had cursed her.

He was the reason she was trapped in this world. The reason she might never see her family and friends again. The reason her kingdom might face civil war. Yes, she had many reasons to hate the man, she reminded herself.

She wished he would hurry and return.

Elora focused on her task, but the monotonous work couldn't vanish the occasional pleasant, traitorous, stray thoughts from her mind, no matter how much she fought them.

She was working on one particularly resistant spot when the hair on her arms suddenly stood on end. She felt a presence behind her. Someone was watching her.

She jerked around to see the menacing shadow crawl across the stone floor toward her. It rose from the ground a few feet away and stood tall, an oblong, shapeless thing. Without warning, it lunged at her.

She dropped to the ground and rolled to the side, barely missing its onslaught. She grabbed the poker and turned. It hovered behind her for a second before it lunged at her again.

She swung the poker at the thing. The metal passed through the apparition, scattering it like mist. She scrambled to her feet. Turning quickly, her eyes went wide, shooting all around the room.

There it was. It swooshed toward her again, passing through her like a ghost. She felt the pressure of its passing as if it had tried to rip her soul out when it exited her body.

Elora stumbled and fell back against the wall. She frantically searched the area, but it was gone. Still, she didn't move for several minutes. Finally, she sank to the ground, her eyes wild, the fireplace poker clutched tightly in her hands. That is how Thorn found her when he entered the castle.

Thorn appeared in the middle of the town as usual. He wasted no time getting to the castle. He saw the rock wall blocking the entrance as he approached. That was good. If the rock wall appeared on both sides, it likely had absorbed all the barrier's power. But it posed a problem. How was he to get inside?

He walked up to the blocked entrance, considering. The dream had always pulled him here since it was centered around Elora. Therefore, he should still be able to get in. He reached out to touch the surface, but his hand passed through it. Well, he could get inside, but what did that mean for the wall's effectiveness?

He stepped into the wall and felt only slight resistance before coming out on the other side. A small motion caught his attention, and he looked down to see the human huddled on the floor, clasping her weapon. He squatted down beside her.

"What's wrong?"

Elora stiffened when she saw him. Her usual stubbornness rose to the surface. He could see it in her eyes. She stood to her feet and brushed off her gown. Whatever had happened, she wasn't about to tell him. Fine, he thought, though he found himself more curious than he should be. A little worried as well. He would need to know if anything was wrong so he could factor it into his plans, he told himself. His concern had nothing to do with the safety of the human.

Without a word, Elora handed him the fireplace poker and took up her usual perch on the stairs. He turned and got to work, chipping away at the wall. The girl had made some progress in his absence. He should be able to break through that night.

"If you could go back in time, would you do things any differently?"

Elora's voice was nearly drowned out by the clinking of metal against stone, but Thorn heard her. At first, he didn't reply, his emotions swirling from anger to stubbornness to guilt. He didn't like that she made him feel guilt.

"I'm trying to break the curse now, aren't I?" His voice had more heat in it than he'd intended, but he didn't apologize.

"Yes, but... Is that because you regret your actions or because you want to prevent war?"

"Why would I regret my actions?" he said with a huff.

Elora sat quietly for several moments before asking, "Why did you do it?"

"Don't you know?"

"I've heard rumors, but I want to hear it from you."

"Your father caused the death of my brother." He slammed the poker into the wall, and a large chunk of stone crashed to the ground.

"But I didn't."

Thorn paused briefly before continuing his work. The clink, clink, clink echoed across the cavernous foyer.

"No, you didn't," he finally replied.

"Tell me about your brother."

"No."

Elora fanned her skirts out on the stair and lifted her hem to stare at her shoes. After a few moments, they began to change to a bright blue. Then, she concentrated on her dress until it matched.

"I never had a brother. Or a sister," she said sadly.

Thorn turned abruptly to face her. "Make no mistake, princess, even though we have a temporary truce, we are not friends." He turned back to the wall and continued his work.

If a look could kill, he would be lying dead on the ground. Without a word, Elora rose gracefully to her feet and glided over to a window as if she wanted to leave him but was too reluctant to do so.

A renewed sense of guilt gnawed at Thorn's insides. The human was right. She hadn't done anything to deserve this. Her parents had already been punished with her loss. And she was stuck here. There was no reason for him to make things worse for her than they already were.

"I looked up to him," he said reluctantly. "I wanted to be just like him someday," he continued.

"What happened to him?" Elora asked curiously.

"I lost him in the war. He saved me from the goblins. We were surrounded. Outnumbered and injured. They almost had me, but he jumped in front of a magical bolt of lightning aimed at me. He sacrificed himself for me. We could not save him. I failed to save him."

"I'm so sorry," Elora said. "But I don't quite understand why you blame my parents if it was goblins that killed him."

He turned and glared at her. "Your parents started the war when they expanded human territory to the mountains, where the goblins lived. They didn't care about the consequences. Elves and goblins have had a long-time feud. Expanding human territory meant forcing them into our lands. They invaded the elven kingdom and destroyed our outlying towns. Killed my people. Killed Ithil," he replied.

"We—I didn't know we caused the war."

"You had not been born yet when it happened. How could you have known?"

Elora sighed.

211

"For what it's worth, I'm sorry the humans caused that much damage. And I'm sorry about your brother," He gave her a quick nod and resumed his work.

Neither of them spoke a word after that. And for a very long time, he was left with his thoughts.

When he had finally removed much of the stone and mortar in the thick wall, he stood back and rammed the handle of the fireplace poker into what remained. Large rocks broke loose and fell at his feet, sending a cloud of dust into the room. He continued until he had opened a hole big enough to walk through.

With a glance at the princess, Thorn stepped through the doorway. And found himself in the upstairs corridor. His howl of frustration and rage was so loud he had no doubt Elora heard him all the way downstairs. He slammed the poker against the wall several times. But it wasn't enough to relieve his turbulent emotions.

He slunk to the ground, his mind racing. What if the plant doesn't work? Or what if it does work on her but doesn't release him? Is there no way out of this? Is he doomed to spend every night for the rest of his long life in this place?

He heard a soft rustling of fabric and glanced up to see Elora walking down the hall. Thankfully, she didn't say anything. She slid to the ground across from him, pulled her knees against her chest and hugged them tightly.

After a while, she spoke. "Thorn?"

He glanced up at her, irritated.

"What?"

"Do you think we can die in here?"

That had his attention. "Why do you ask that?" He remembered how he had found her when he arrived.

She shrugged. "No reason. I was just wondering." She paused and then continued. "Will my body age and die in the real world?"

Is that what was troubling her? "No. You will stay just as you were when the curse took effect. The only way you will die is if someone kills you."

Her eyes opened wide, and she jerked her head up to face him. Apparently, she hadn't thought of that possibility.

"I don't think my family will let that happen." She wrinkled her nose. "So, does that mean that my body is going to lie there asleep generation after generation forever?"

Thorn snorted. "They'll probably put you in a glass coffin on display for everyone to come and marvel at your beauty."

Elora frowned. "No, I don't think they'll do that. More likely, they'll keep me in my room and assign a few people to take care of me."

He pictured her in an elegant human bedchamber, lying on a canopy bed draped in thick curtains, ivy growing up the walls and around the room. He saw her lovely golden hair spread out around her and her face peaceful in sleep. He shook his head to clear away the image and glanced up at the window and the gray sky above.

"But what about in here? Do you think we can die in here?"

He lowered his eyebrows. "Why do you think you might die in here?"

She shrugged nonchalantly. "No reason. You never know. I might fall down the staircase or catch my dress on fire in the fireplace."

He snorted. "Are you usually that clumsy?"

Her lip curled up in a half smile. "No, but you never know."

He gazed back out at the clouds. "I don't know. I suppose it's possible." Then he pulled his dagger from its sheath and cut a small gash in his palm.

Elora dropped her knees and scooted over to him. "What are you doing?!" She grabbed his hand and used the bottom of her skirt to wipe the blood off his palm. She raised her eyes to his in horror. "You're bleeding."

He nodded. "A person can get injured in here. And if injured, then... I suggest you be careful."

He didn't need to say any more. Elora's face paled, and again he wondered what had happened prior to his arrival. But before he could insist she tell him, he felt himself begin to fade. "Be careful," was all he had time to say before he awoke.

A tired-looking messenger rushed into the elven throne room and bowed before the king. The king motioned for the man to rise, and a servant walked over to him and took the parchment he held out.

"A message from the king of Yeatton, Your Majesty."

The servant handed the parchment to the king, and he opened it. A scowl formed on his face as he read.

With an angry growl, he threw the paper to the ground. "Bring me Mage Elion!"

Murmurs arose from the nobles in court as they waited for the mage's arrival, but the king said nothing else. He sat with his elbow on the armrest and his chin propped up on his hand. His eyes stared into space, barely blinking.

Finally, Mage Elion arrived and bowed before the king.

"Have you heard from Mage Thornindell?" he asked.

"No, Your Majesty, but he should be nearing the end of his quest. I predict that he'll arrive in the Kingdom of Yeatton in another day or two."

"Well, he won't be greeted kindly there," the king said with a huff.

"What do you mean, Your Majesty?"

"The king of Yeatton has just sent me a message. It says the goblins told them their spies had discovered that our proposed cure for the curse was a hoax. That we are using this trick to gain their trust and invade the kingdom. They even accuse us of planning to kill the princess when we pretend to cure her." He clenched his jaw. "They say that no elf is welcome in their kingdom, and they have subsequently declared war against us."

Elion gasped. "They will kill Thorn on sight."

"Yes. All we can do is try to get a message to him. He should get the plant, in case we have an opportunity to use it in the future, and return here immediately."

"Yes, Your Majesty." Elion gave him a quick bow and hurried out.

Chapter 14

Thoughts of Elora plagued Thorn as he made his way through the dark cave tunnels. What was she scared of? Why did she ask if she could die there? He had gone over everything he could recall about the curse, and nothing stood out. There wasn't much to know. Except... Something sat in his mind out of reach. Something he had read once during his lessons. It was about the man who had created the curse. Yes, he had disappeared.

Thorn dug around in his memory for the information. Mage Fallinon, a renegade mage, had created the curse to use on a member of the royal family. It was said that when he cast the curse, something went wrong, and he vanished. Nothing happened to the royal, but the mage was never seen again.

Changes had been made to the spell over the years, improving it, making it safer. For, even though using such spells was frowned upon, it wasn't illegal. Mages were simply expected to employ wisdom when making such a decision. Wisdom he was now willing to admit he had lacked.

Could Fallinon's curse have backfired and trapped him in the dream world? Thorn shifted the bow and quiver strapped to his back and bent to avoid the low overhang as he squeezed around the tight corner in the small cave passage.

He understood how easy it was to make a mistake with a spell. If Fallinon had inadvertently trapped himself in his own curse, he couldn't still be there. Could he? Thorn called to mind the strange wind he had felt when first attempting to change the barrier magic. Was Elora in danger?

He stopped and stared into the darkness ahead. Should he return early? He didn't like the sense of urgency that crept through his bones. She'll be fine, he told himself. Not that he cared. He pushed the thoughts away, but as he passed on through the maze of tunnels and caverns, dodging stalactites and stalagmites, the sense of danger and worry stayed with him, just below the surface, picking at him and nibbling at him like a legion of hungry fleas.

When he began nearing the other side of the mountain, he heard the slightest whisper in the air. He extinguished his light and listened. Someone was there. He could hear them breathing. He emptied his mind of everything except his training. With his back pushed against the wall, he crept forward, silent as a ghost. When he reached the corner, he knelt and slowly peered around the boulder.

A goblin sentry stood there, his bored gaze locked on a bat sleeping on the wall beside him. Thorn eased himself around the rock, staying low. Pulling his dagger from his belt, careful not to make a sound, he moved around behind the goblin, using the boulders for cover whenever he could.

He couldn't see as well as goblins could in the cave's darkness, but he could hear even better. And a soft glow coming from a cavern behind his enemy provided all the light he needed. The goblin didn't even realize he was there until the blood began gushing out of his neck. Thorn clasped his hand over the man's mouth just in case he managed to make a noise, but there was no need. He had been very efficient.

As the life bled out of him, Thorn slowly lowered him to the ground. Clearly, the goblin wasn't alone. This could be a problem since this passage was the only one on his map.

Thorn crept down the tunnel and hid behind another boulder at the opening of a small cave. Staying low, he glanced into the stone room. Five goblins sat around a small fire, eating their evening meal. Thorn moved back into the tunnel and pulled out his short swords. Daggers might work better in such close quarters, but he liked his chances more with his swords. They lacked the length of his long blade, so they should do the job fine.

He wasn't too concerned, though, he would prefer to engage them in the opening, where he could better use his magic. He was about to go rushing in when one of them spoke.

"Here. Take this plate to Orik."

He heard one of them shuffle to their feet, and he quickly retreated to where he had left the goblin. He grabbed the body and shoved it behind a boulder, taking the place of the dead sentry. It wouldn't fool the goblin for long, but it might be long enough.

The man strolled up to him, but he kept his back turned.

"Orik. Here's your dinner."

Thorn reached out and took the plate without turning around. He placed it carefully on the boulder.

The last thing he needed was for it to drop to the ground and alert the others.

"Hey! You're not Orik!"

Thorn's hand shot out like a snake, stabbing his blade into the man's throat. He quickly caught him and lowered his body to the ground like the other.

Thorn hurried quietly back to the cave. Only four now. He liked those odds even better. Thorn took a deep breath and then launched himself into the cave. The goblins looked up in shock and scrambled to their feet, hurriedly reaching for their weapons. He had run his blade through the heart of one of them before they could react. The goblin fell with a guttural cry, and Thorn swiftly pulled his sword free.

The remaining three goblins, their eyes filled with anger and fear, leaped into action. They muttered incantations under their breath, and their bodies shimmered with a strange magical energy. They instantly transformed into a trio of grotesque creatures—half-human, half-beast monstrosities, their claws and fangs bared.

Thorn, undeterred, stepped back, his elemental magic at the ready. Flames ignited around his fingertips as he prepared to counter their offensive. One of them lunged at him from the right, its jagged claws aimed at his chest. Thorn twisted his body with elven grace, narrowly avoiding the attack, and sent a searing burst of fire toward the man. The flames engulfed him as another of the goblins attacked from the left and the last from behind.

The goblin howled in agony before reverting to its goblin form, its charred body collapsing to the ground, but Thorn paid it no heed. His attention focused on the

219

last two. They had transformed again. Into beings not so easily susceptible to fire. One of them, a massive, hulking brute with thick, armored skin, swung a heavy club-like arm toward Thorn. At the same time, the other, a shadowy, ethereal form, darted around the elf, attacking in a haphazard, unpredictable manner.

Thorn leaped backward, narrowly escaping the crushing blow of the first and deftly dodged the second. With a flick of his wrist, he summoned a gust of wind, sending the enormous monster tumbling backward, its transformation disrupted. He found the other somewhat more difficult to defeat. He skillfully parried the goblin's ethereal strikes, waiting for an opportunity. As the goblin materialized briefly to attack, Thorn seized the opening and slashed his short sword across its throat. It gurgled in surprise, transforming back into its goblin form as it clutched its wound, blood pouring from its neck.

The last goblin howled in rage, quickly jumping back to his feet. *Idiot*, thought Thorn. It lunged at the elf with a reckless charge, attempting to avenge its fallen comrades. Thorn met the attack head-on, his short swords a blur of deadly grace. He deflected the goblin's strikes and disarmed it with a swift twist of his wrist.

Cornered and weaponless, the goblin resorted to its transformative magic once more. It morphed into a giant, venomous snake, its fangs dripping with lethal poison.

The serpent struck with lightning speed, but Thorn was ready. He evaded the snake's bite by a hair's breadth, and with a well-aimed strike, he severed its head from its body. He didn't even glance back as the snake morphed back into its goblin form and fell, lifeless, to the ground.

Thorn wiped the blood from his short swords on the shirt of the nearest goblin body. Without sparing the goblins another glance, he sheathed the swords and continued his journey.

As he suspected, the goblin's cave stood only a short distance from the tunnel entrance. Thorn emerged. The darkness of the cloudy night was only slightly brighter than the cave. He had been in there all day and for a good bit of the night.

As he headed into the tree line, a magical tracker bird flew up to him, a small piece of parchment held tightly in its foot. It landed on Thorn's shoulder and dematerialized when Thorn removed the letter. He unfolded the paper and read the king's message. With an angry growl, he wadded the page and threw it in the air, burning it with fire before it hit the ground.

His plans didn't change. They may have become more complicated, but they didn't change.

He needed to make camp soon. He had been in the caves too long. But he didn't feel comfortable sleeping this near to a goblin post.

He traveled for another hour. Probably not as long as he should have, but he had begun to worry about Elora. He didn't even deny it anymore. Something scared her, and the thought had been simmering inside him all day. He needed to check on her.

Thorn didn't take the time to build a fire or even to clean the blood off himself. But he did take the precaution of climbing the tallest tree he could see and perching in its branches. In goblin territory, this would

be considerably safer than sleeping on the ground. In no
time, he fell asleep.

Elora felt it again. That shadowy presence. It was
watching her. Her eyes shot around, looking for it, her
hands clasped tightly around the fireplace poker.

Her heart pounded in her chest as she scanned the
room, trying to pinpoint the source of her unease. She
backed into a corner, hoping that would mean she only
had to worry about threats from the front. But it was a
shadow. Who knew what it could do? Movement out of
the corner of her eye caught her attention.

A growing cloud of darkness was there, coalescing
from the muted surroundings. It began to take shape,
becoming darker and more substantial, like ink
spreading in water. Fear gripped Elora as she
recognized the impending threat. The shadow was
about to attack.

Gripping her weapon tightly, she steadied herself,
her knuckles white against the wrought iron. The
shadow seemed to hesitate momentarily, its form
wavering as if gauging her resolve. Then, with a sudden
surge of malevolence, it lunged toward her.

Elora swung the poker with all her strength, but it
was like trying to strike smoke. The poker passed
through the shadow without resistance as if it were
nothing more than an illusion. Panic welled up within
her as she turned to face the approaching darkness
again, but it was too late.

The shadow engulfed her, and Elora felt an icy chill
course through her body. It was as if a piece of her soul

had been torn away. She screamed in pain, clutching her chest, but the shadow showed no mercy. It seemed to revel in her agony, its shape growing even darker and more defined as it fed on her suffering.

Desperation gave her strength. Elora frantically scrambled away from the apparition, using the fireplace poker to push herself up from the ground where she had fallen. She watched in horror as the dark shape loomed over her, its features becoming sharper, more corporeal with each passing moment.

In that instant, she realized the pattern. The shadow grew stronger just before it attacked. It was as if it needed her fear and pain to materialize fully. Determination replaced her terror as she made her stand. She wouldn't give it what it wanted.

As the apparition descended upon her again, Elora forced herself to focus. She willed herself not to flinch, not to scream. She held her ground and watched as the shadow's darkness wavered, struggling to maintain its form without her fear to sustain it.

And then, just as the shadow was about to envelop her, she struck. The weapon again passed through the ghostly form, but this time, she felt a slight resistance, a subtle shift in its consistency. The shadow let out an eerie, guttural growl. It seemed like her attacks were having an effect, albeit a minor one.

Elora didn't back down. She swung the poker again, this time with even more force. The dark cloud, its shape wavering, seemed to recoil in response. Encouraged by this, Elora continued her assault, striking at the menacing presence repeatedly.

The shadow grew darker, more defined, and less ethereal with each hit. Elora realized that she was slowly driving it back, causing it to lose its spectral nature. But it fought back with a growing rage, its threatening aura intensifying.

Just as Elora felt a glimmer of hope, the shadow launched a sudden and vicious attack. It flowed forward with an unexpected ferocity, striking her before she could react. With a final surge of hostility, it lunged one last time. Elora tried to hit it again, but their previous struggle had drained her strength.

The shadow collided with her, and this time, she felt its cold tendrils wrap around her like a vice. Pain seared through her body as it tore into her, leaving her bruised and battered. Elora's dress was ripped, her skin scraped and bleeding. She gasped for breath as the shadow seemed to feed on her suffering once more.

Then, as suddenly as it had attacked, the shadow withdrew, leaving Elora trembling and injured on the foyer floor. She watched as it dissipated into the washed-out surroundings, fading into nothingness.

Elora's breath came in quick, pained bursts as she stumbled to the stairs. She lowered herself down and hugged her bruised ribs. With all her heart, she wished Thorn were there.

"Who did this to you!" Thorn's eyes flashed with fury when he saw Elora's injuries, and his hands clenched her shoulders possessively. He would kill them! Whoever had dared hurt her would die the most painful death he could imagine. Elora's heart warmed at the passionate rage that radiated off him in waves. Did he really care for her? A human?

She gasped as his hands gently ran over her body, searching for damage. It would have felt incredible if she hadn't been in so much pain. She struggled to find her voice, her eyes filled with tears of both pain and relief.

"It was—the shadow," she managed to croak out, her voice barely above a whisper.

Thorn listened intently as Elora recounted her harrowing encounter with the wispy form.

Once he was satisfied that her injuries, though painful, weren't life-threatening, Thorn's focus shifted to the assailant. "Fallinon," he muttered, almost to himself.

Elora blinked, surprised. "Fallinon? Do you know what that shadow is?"

"It must be him. He's the mage who created the sleeping curse. It appears he got trapped here when he tried to use it on someone else."

Elora winced as she shifted to a more comfortable position. "You could be right. Whatever it is, it's like he's a part of this dream world, and he doesn't want anyone to disturb his cursed slumber."

"Then it's time to wake him up and put an end to this nightmare." Thorn's expression darkened even further, and his eyes darted around the room. "Where is it now?" he asked, his voice like steel, low and dangerous. Elora could only show him where it had been when it disappeared.

"Fallinon!" Thorn roared, his voice echoing through the castle. "Show yourself, you coward! Or do you only attack helpless females!" Elora bristled a little at the reference to 'helpless females,' but she didn't comment.

Tingles ran through her. Tingles of fear. Tingles of excitement. She couldn't deny that she liked this Thorn.

This ferocious, frightening warrior fighting to defend her. His blood-stained clothes only added to his fierce appearance.

The castle seemed to respond to Thorn's command, its walls shifting and changing as if reacting to his call. Elora watched in awe as the surroundings transformed. Everything grew hazy and regained its original gray-scale coloring. Darkness loomed, making it difficult for her human eyes to see. Thankfully, Thorn didn't seem to have the same problem.

The shadowy presence emerged from the blackness surrounding them, its form taking shape and growing darker with each passing moment. But this time, it faced a fully armed, enraged elf warrior, not a frightened human with a fireplace poker. Thorn pulled out his short swords and stormed over to the mass of smoke and fog.

"Fallinon," he called out, his voice dripping with contempt. "Show yourself. It's time to pay for the curse you've wrought."

The apparition, sensing strength in its adversary, let out a guttural growl of frustration. It floated above them both, tendrils of shadow flashing out to the sides like the arms of an octopus.

"Are you too frightened to show your true form?" Thorn laughed derisively at it. "Come on, Fallinon, let the lady see the true appearance of an elf who has betrayed his kind."

The smoke began to shape itself, growing longer and more substantial. Arms and legs sprouted, and a head formed with long hair and sharp ears. In mere moments, the wispy form of a man holding a long broadsword stood before them.

"Betrayed my kind?! It was not I who wronged our people that fateful day. It was him! That sniveling, conniving royal, Nuadrid!" Fallinon's voice blew through the air like the wind of a storm. "I tried to set things right!"

"That is not what history tells."

Fallinon roared. "What do I care for history!"

"I might be willing to believe you," Thorn said, his voice hard but calm, as he eased himself around the shadowy man to stand between him and Elora. He gently pushed her back, and she went, hurrying over to the corner of the room. "If it weren't for the fact that you attacked Elora."

Fallinon's voice was thunder. "A human! They are even worse than the royals. They are mere insects. Worth no more than to be trampled underfoot. How dare she invade my dream world and treat it as if it were her own."

"She may be a human," Thorn said, stepping closer to the apparition, "but she's my human. And no one harms what is mine!"

Elora's heart leaped into her throat at his words. She struggled to breathe, her hands clasped tightly. She gasped when Thorn lunged at the phantom elf, her wide eyes following his every move.

The clash between Thorn and Fallinon was fierce and relentless. But Thorn's weapons sliced through the shadowy form as often as they collided with it. As if sensing an opportunity, Fallinon increased his strikes.

He surged forward with evil intent, attempting to envelop Thorn. The elf mage reacted quickly, spinning away with fluid grace.

Fallinon's form shifted and twisted like a wraith. Thorn parried each attack, the clash of metal against magical mist causing eerie sparks to fly. He could feel the shadow's growing resistance, his substance no longer as ephemeral as before.

Elora watched the battle unfold, her heart pounding with anxiety. She knew Thorn was a formidable warrior, but Fallinon seemed relentless, always returning after each strike.

"Thorn, it grows darker just before it attacks!" Elora shouted, trying to help as much as she could. "That's when you can hurt it!"

Fallinon growled at her interference and surged toward the princess.

"No, you don't!" roared Thorn, blocking his path.

Fallinon had darkened in preparation for his attack on the human, and Thorn didn't miss the opportunity. He sliced through the phantom's arm. The shadow let out a piercing shriek, its form writhing and contorting in agony. It recoiled, retreating into the room's shadows, its shape flickering and fading.

Thorn pursued the disgraced elf, his swords poised for the final blow. "You can't escape me," he hissed.

Fallinon, his menacing presence greatly diminished, tried one last desperate attack. He surged forward with renewed intensity, his form growing impossibly dark.

Thorn raised one of his swords over his head and stopped the descent of the wraith blade while he plunged the other into Fallinon's heart.

A final, otherworldly wail filled the chamber as the shadow dissipated into nothingness. Thorn stood victorious, his chest heaving with exertion.

Elora couldn't contain her relief and joy. She threw herself into Thorn's arms, ignoring the pain in her bruised body. "You did it!"

Thorn held her close, his expression softened with relief and affection. How had he ever hated this girl?

Suddenly, realizing what she had done, Elora jumped back. She cleared her throat and ran her hands down the skirt of her dress.

"Sorry," she said sheepishly.

Thorn studied her closely, his face unreadable.

"There's nothing to be sorry for."

She watched as he faded away, waking up in the real world. She stood motionless for a long time, breathing heavily, eyes roaming the lingering darkness. The silence beat against her ears.

She relived the fight in her mind over and over again. Finally, she moved to the library and fell into a chair by the fire. The faint color had already returned to the world here, so much farther from the epicenter of the shadow's powers.

Elora sat and stared at the flames. The glow of the fire and the crackle of the burning logs comforted her. She stayed there throughout the following day, remembering.

Remembering how Thorn's voice had roared.

Remembering how his eyes had blazed.

Remembering how his muscles had bunched, how his swords had twirled, how he had defeated that monster.

All for her.

He had risked his life to avenge her. Her heart still galloped in her chest, but it was no longer from fear.

Thorn arrived at the base of Mount Morend when the sun was high in the sky the following day. Elora had been on his mind since he awoke. He didn't like leaving her so suddenly. Fallinon was dead. He was sure of that. But she had been injured. True, he had checked her injuries himself, and none had been severe, but still...

He didn't like leaving her so suddenly after what had happened. He had lain there for a time, trying to fall back asleep, but finally gave up and resumed his journey.

He pulled a magic tracker from his pack. Elion had spelled it for him before he left. If it worked correctly, it should take him straight to a Helvola plant, provided he was no more than a mile away from one.

He walked all along the western side of the base of the mountain. There was no response from the tracker for the longest time. He almost began to despair. But then he began to sense a pull from a small cave to his right. It was definitely the plant.

The blue petals of the Helvola were luminescent, glowing a beautiful turquoise against the darkness of the cave. He removed it from its roots carefully. He pulled a vial and a mortar and pestle from his pack. Using his elemental powers, he quickly dried the petals and then crushed them with the pestle.

Pouring in the liquid from the vial he carried, he stirred the mixture with magic and refilled the empty vial with the resulting potion. He gently wrapped it back in its cloth and replaced it in his pack. Now, he just had to get this to her safely.

Thorn closed his eyes and concentrated on Elora's castle. He had been there before, when he cursed her, but even if he hadn't, he had visited it so many times in his dreams that he had no trouble envisioning it. Within a blink, he dematerialized from the cave and rematerialized in the Kingdom of Yeatton.

Frink, goblin Vrek's youngest brother, angrily kicked a stone by his foot. Why was he the one stuck here watching for the elf mage? He wanted to be inside training with the rest of the warriors.

He snorted. The stupid humans still didn't realize they had an entire goblin platoon hiding in their basement, waiting for its opportunity to kill their beloved princess.

Frink adjusted his human guard uniform and wrinkled his human-looking nose. He wasn't convinced the elf would show up at this spot even if he did come. It was too much out in the open. He must know that the humans hated them now more than ever. Surely, he wouldn't appear in so exposed a place. He didn't care what Vrek had said about him having to appear where he had been before. That was nothing but an excuse to send his kid brother on a useless mission.

The young goblin blinked in disbelief when the air in the center of the courtyard began to shimmer. He rubbed his eyes as it grew thicker, coalescing into a man. An elf! He took off into the castle. The elf was here. It was time to put their plan into action.

Chapter 15

T horn lay low under an abandoned carriage a stone's throw from the castle. The number of guards that patrolled the castle gates had increased significantly since he'd last been there. But that wouldn't prove too great a challenge. However, he wanted to get in with as little bloodshed as possible, so he decided to use stealth instead of force.

He had been spying on the guards for a couple of hours, noting their rounds and the time it took them to make them. He should have stayed and observed longer, but a sense of urgency almost overpowered him. There was only the briefest moment after the first group rounded the far corner before the next group rounded the near corner. It wouldn't give him much time. He would have to be quick.

As he waited, a group of men hurrying toward the castle kitchens caught his eye. There was nothing odd in their appearance, but something seemed off. He cast his magic out towards them, and what he saw made his skin crawl. Goblins, using a glamor to appear human. What were goblins doing there?

He remembered the letter from the king. Goblins had convinced King Leopold that elves were trying to kill Elora. What better way to gain allies in the war than to have elves do just that?

They were going to transform themselves into elves and kill her. He'd bet his life on it. At least they were going to try. They would have to get through him first.

Thorn called up mist from the air and spread it over the courtyard. It didn't quite fit that time of the day, but he needed some cover. A few guards glanced toward the strange phenomenon suspiciously, but no outcry was given.

Thorn's heart pounded in his chest. He wanted to run to Elora's room and make sure she was alright, but he knew his only chance lay in caution. So, he casually meandered across the courtyard and to the kitchens, following the group of goblin men.

The kitchen was abuzz with activity. Thorn covered his ears with his hair and tucked the long strands into his collar before entering the bustling room. He would never make it to Elora in time if he were recognized and the guards were called.

He measured his pace through the kitchen so as to not cause any suspicion. The goblins had already disappeared down the hallway. He rushed to catch up as soon as he made it away from prying human eyes.

Thorn felt an almost overwhelming desire to take out the group then and there, but he didn't dare risk it. He didn't know how many others there were and where they were positioned. If any of them were already near the sleeping princess, they could attack before he reached them if he was delayed by fighting. So, he followed them, grinding his teeth the whole way.

To his surprise, their disguises fell when the goblins stepped into the hallway leading to the princess's chambers. He knew their magic had not timed out because goblins could hold their glamours for days. It appeared more as if it had suddenly been cut off or smothered.

Thorn was both pleased and annoyed at this revelation. It meant that the king wasn't only taking physical precautions, but he was taking magical precautions as well. Without magic, the goblin's ruse would be more difficult to enact, if not impossible. But this magical suppression barrier would also make it more difficult for him to fight so many people simultaneously since he wouldn't be able to access the elements.

The moment the goblin's magic cloaks fell, the guards sprang into action.

"Intruders," someone shouted.

The call echoed down the hall as several guards converged on them. But the goblins weren't looking at the guards.

"Elf," one of them hissed when they sighted Thorn, their eyes seething with hatred.

"You have the princess to thank for your lives," he said through clenched teeth as they took up defensive positions.

The goblins, cunning creatures that they were, managed to slip one of their number past the oncoming guards in the commotion while the other two remained.

Thorn saw red. There was so much that one goblin could do while they wasted time, fighting.

Ten guards were in the foyer with him and the goblins, all brandishing weapons.

It wouldn't have been much trouble for him to end all of them with his magic, but without that, and considering that he didn't want to hurt the princess's men while they were only trying to protect her, this would be much more difficult.

He pulled out his long sword, sheath and all. He would focus on blocking their attacks. His blade was sharp, and he didn't want to hurt anyone accidentally, but he would draw it if he had to.

There was a beat of quiet before the foyer erupted. As he blocked and parried strikes from the guards, dodging, ducking, and dancing around his foes, he noticed that the goblins were not being engaged. The guards blocked them from proceeding up the hallway, but none fought them.

Apparently, the guards didn't feel they proposed quite as much of a risk as an elf did, though they didn't seem to trust them completely.

The steel of the guards' swords clanged against Thorn's scabbard relentlessly.

He knew he had to end the fight as soon as possible. None of them had the luxury of time. Especially not Elora, with the third goblin absent from the melee.

In no time, the guards had forgotten about the goblins as all of them, goblins included, converged on the elf.

Thorn tried to hold up as best as he could physically, but there was no overpowering ten trained guards and two villainous goblins with nothing but his wits and a sheathed sword.

He knew he would either have to resort to magic or unsheathe his sword.

As the guards focused all their attention on him, the goblins saw a chance to escape and took it. Through the commotion, he saw them push open the wide doors and slip into the room.

"Idiot humans," he grunted. How could the guards have left the doors unattended just to engage in a useless fight? His stomach churned with his helplessness. He had to do something, even if it meant killing these men.

The pommel of his sword came down one of the guards' heads, and the man crumpled to the ground, unconscious. If only he had more time, he could do the same to the others, but he didn't have time.

Choosing the best of his limited options, Thorn began to inch his way back toward the end of the hall, where he knew the magic suppression didn't reach.

Thinking he was attempting to escape, the guards followed him persistently. He moved back until he was sure all of them had left the no-magic zone.

Then he conjured up a mighty wind, swirling it into a cyclone. The men's feet lifted off the floor, and they spun around wildly in the air. Thorn expanded the cyclone's reach to spread across the hall and down the stairs. Anyone who tried to enter that space would be swept up into it. With a bubble of air surrounding him, Thorn rushed through the flying and thrashing men. Their cries of panic and outrage followed him down the hallway.

Scattered shouts and running footsteps from other parts of the palace signaled to him that more guards were on their way. He did not dare hesitate in case some came from another direction.

Thorn ran to the princess's rooms and opened the wide doors in time to see the last two human guards drop to the ground. One of the goblins rushed over to the princess, dagger drawn.

"Stop!" cried Thorn, pulling his sword free and throwing the scabbard to the side.

The goblin quickly placed the dagger against Elora's neck.

"Why should we, elf?"

"Your ruse has failed. The humans have seen you for what you are."

"None in this room will live."

A whimper in the corner of the room attracted Thorn's attention. A human girl pushed herself back against the window, grabbing the curtains with frightened hands. Blood ran down her arm, and a large bruise was forming on her cheek.

Thorn growled. "And what about the guards in the hall? They know you are here."

"We will simply tell them that we came to protect the princess from you. As we speak, dozens of our men are downstairs disguised as elves, taking on other guards. After we kill the princess, this pathetic human girl, and you. There will be no one to say any differently." He pressed the knife harder against Elora's throat, and a bead of blood formed.

Thorn held out his hand toward her. "But!" he said, stopping the progress of the knife. "They won't believe you."

Thorn saw the human girl stealthily inch toward the fireplace. What was she doing? She would get herself killed. And Elora. He adjusted his position, lowering his sword to the ground in a gesture of peace. The goblin by Elora relaxed somewhat, easing the pressure of his weapon.

When Thorn rose, he clasped his hands behind his back, slowly reaching for the dagger hidden there.

Thankfully, the stupid goblins had yet to search him. They hadn't even secured his arms. They were probably too frightened to approach him, thought Thorn with an internal smirk.

The goblin's eyes narrowed, and his lips formed into a tight line. "Why won't they believe us?"

"Think about it," Thorn said, closing his hands around the weapon. "You three will be standing here, relatively unharmed, while two guards, a woman, and an elf warrior lie dead on the floor. Do you really think the humans will believe your story?"

Doubt appeared in the goblin's eyes. He glanced at the other two, all three of them uneasy.

While the goblins' attention was diverted, Thorn pulled the dagger and threw it with expert precision. Before it even landed, embedded in the goblin's skull, he retrieved his sword and sprang on the other two. They grasped their weapons tightly, panic spreading across their faces. They had expected this mission to be easy. They hadn't counted on him. With a few deft moves, the elf quickly dispatched them. They were no match for his rage.

As the last goblin fell, Thorn turned his eyes to the bed. The human girl stood between him and it. Her hands trembled, shaking the fireplace poker she held, but her eyes burned fiercely. What was it about human women and fireplace pokers?

"I'm not going to hurt her," said Thorn, sliding his blade back into its scabbard. He held up his hands as he slowly approached.

"Then, why are you here?" she said, her voice quivering with fear.

"I am here to awaken her."

That reply obviously caught her off guard. She lowered the poker slightly, softening her defenses. "How?"

He kept one hand raised while he slowly pulled his pack off with the other. "I have brought a potion made from the Helvola plant. It is said to be able to cure all injuries." He opened the bag and pulled out the bottle while the girl watched curiously, but she didn't move from her position.

"How can I trust you?"

"If I wanted her dead, do you think she would still live?" he asked with a raised brow.

The girl frowned but finally moved away.

"Alright, but if you so much as look like you're trying to hurt her, I'll run you through." She waved the poker threateningly.

Thorn chuckled and shook his head as he approached Elora. She looked so helpless lying there.

So peaceful.

So beautiful.

He unwrapped the vial and started to remove the stopper, but he hesitated.

"What are you waiting for," the girl asked nervously.

"I want to try something else first," he said.

Thorn leaned in and pressed his lips to hers in the most chaste of kisses. A gasp sounded behind him as her eyes gently fluttered open.

Just then, the door burst in, and a group of guards stormed into the room.

"Wait!" shouted the girl, moving between him and the guards. Thorn hardly registered the irony. His focus was on the girl lying before him.

A smile split his face as she blinked and glanced around, clearly confused. "Thorn? What happened? Why are we in my bedroom?" She sat up and noticed the girl and the guards crowding in the space. Murmurs spread through their ranks and out into the hall, where they became yells. More footsteps rushed toward them, but neither Thorn nor Elora paid any attention to any of it.

"The plant worked?" she asked him.

The human girl danced up beside the bed. "He didn't use the plant," she said with a giggle. "He kissed you."

Thorn finally placed her voice and turned to her. "You must be Deanna."

The girl's eyes widened in surprise. "How did you know that?"

Thorn reached out and helped Elora to her feet. "How could I ever forget such a charming singing voice?"

Deanna burst out laughing just as the king and queen pushed past the guards and into the room.

"It is true?" asked the queen, craning to see over the taller men.

"Mother," Elora rushed into her arms as the men moved out of their way.

Thorn stood to the side and watched as people came from nowhere to greet their beloved princess. Soon, the room was too small to hold them all. The queen and king pulled Elora out into the hall. She tried to protest, looking back at him, but he waved her on. They would have time to talk later.

"Um."

Thorn turned to see a guard watching him warily.

241

"If you would be so kind as to remove the cyclone."

"Of course," he replied with a chuckle.

Thorn sat with Elora on the edge of the fountain in the castle gardens. A mist surrounded them, sparkling in the torchlight. The last day had been a whirlwind of activity for Elora but a relatively peaceful one for him. A bit boring, actually.

He had been given a room in the castle, had a short meeting with Elora's father, and had sent a letter to his king in Allanar, but other than that, he had been pretty much left alone. He had spent most of his time exercising, wishing he could talk to the princess. But her people had needed to see her. He understood that.

So, he had waited.

After a bountiful feast, at which the king introduced him to the people, a ball was in full swing. Many things still needed to be worked out between the elves and the humans, and it would take a while for the humans to accept him. Still, as he thought about Elion's story over the campfire that night, he felt like he was making good progress healing some of the damage between their peoples.

Many men lined up to dance with the princess, but Thorn grabbed her hand and pulled her out into the garden. He was tired of waiting. They needed to talk.

Finally, they were together.

Finally, they were alone.

Elora smiled shyly at him. They both understood what it meant that he could wake her, but the feeling was so new and strange.

Thorn reached up and ran his knuckles down the side of her face, staring deeply into her eyes. Red colored her cheeks, and she lowered her gaze to her lap.

"No," he said gently, lifting her chin. He tilted his head, examining her face, and she glanced away nervously.

"What is it?" she asked, her voice a whisper in the night air.

"I wondered how you would look in the real world. In full color. You are even more beautiful than I imagined."

Elora blushed again, and he chuckled. "I like this color on you."

"Stop," she protested. "I must look a fright." She lifted her hand to her hair and tried to smooth it out. Why had they sat here? The fountain was beautiful, but the damp did horrible things to her hair.

He gently took her wrist and pulled her hand away. "Don't," he said. "You look perfect as you are, frizzy hair and all."

Thorn leaned in, his hand cupping her head. His lips brushed against hers, soft and gentle at first. Then firmer, harder, more demanding. Elora threw her arms around his neck, her hands tangling in the long strands of his hair.

He pulled her closer, his body hard and unyielding. The way his lips moved against hers awakened something deep inside her.

This was where she belonged.

Here in his arms.

She had finally found love.

The End

Thank you for taking the time to read one of my books! I'm enjoying writing this series. I've had a love for fairytales ever since I was a child, and "Sleeping Beauty" was always my favorite. Then *The Lord of the Rings* entered my life, and my love of elves and all things elvish grew. It's been amazing combining the two!

It would just thrill me to pieces if you would leave a review of this book on Goodreads or your favorite bookstore's website. I enjoy reading them. It makes me feel just a little bit more connected to all of you out there who share my love of reading and love of fantasy. Thanks in advance.